W9-CAY-512

Destination Gold!

JULIE LAWSON

DESTINATION GOLD!

ORCA BOOK PUBLISHERS

Canadian Cataloguing in Publication Data
Lawson, Julie, 1947–
Destination gold!

ISBN 1-55143-155-6 (bound) – ISBN 1-55143-157-2 (pbk.)

1. Klondike River Valley (Yukon)—Gold discoveries–Juvenile fiction. I. Title.
PS8573.A94D47 2000 jC813'.54   C00-910805-X   PZ7.L43828De 2000

First published in the United States, 2001

Library of Congress Catalog Card Number: 00-105894

Orca Book Publishers gratefully acknowledges the support for our publishing programs provided by the following agencies: The Government of Canada through the Book Publishing Industry Development Program (BPIDP), The Canada Council for the Arts, and the British Columbia Arts Council.

Cover illustration by Ken Campbell, Imagecraft Studio Ltd.
Cover design by Christine Toller
Printed and bound in Canada

IN CANADA:
Orca Book Publishers
PO Box 5626, Station B
Victoria, BC Canada
V8R 6S4

IN THE UNITED STATES:
Orca Book Publishers
PO Box 468
Custer, WA USA
98240-0468

02 01 00 • 5 4 3 2 1

For Guy — for being in the right place at the right time.

. Author's Note .

On August 17, 1896, acting on a tip from prospector Robert Henderson, three men — George Carmack, Skookum Jim Mason and Dawson Charlie — made an enormous gold discovery on Rabbit Creek, a tributary of the Klondike River. Within two weeks, all of the creek — renamed Bonanza — had been staked.

As winter was closing in, it was almost a full year before news of the discovery reached the outside world. And when two gold-laden steamers arrived in San Francisco and Seattle in July, 1897, the rush was on.

It is estimated that more than 100,000 people set out for the Klondike, with some 40,000 actually making it. Some of these reached Dawson City in the fall of 1897, but the vast majority flooded into the town the summer of 1898. That summer, Dawson became the largest city in North America west of Winnipeg, Manitoba, and north of Seattle, Washington.

The Klondike fever that swept the world was short-lived. By the summer of 1899, Dawson City, the "Queen City of the North," boasted new government buildings and stately homes, complete with running water, electricity and telephones. But by the end of the summer, Dawson was emptied as word came of a gold discovery in Nome, Alaska. Another rush was on.

One hundred years after the Klondike Stampede, in the fall of 1998, I traveled to Dawson City — population 2000 — and struck a different sort of gold. For several months I had the good fortune to experience life in a small, northern community. Living in the heritage house that was author Pierre Berton's childhood home, across the street from Robert Service's cabin and down the road from the Jack London Centre, I was well supplied with literary muses. That fall, and in the winter of 1999, I fell under the spell of the Yukon and immersed myself in the Klondike, both past and present. *Destination Gold!* is the result.

The Dawson City Museum and Archives was an important source in the research of this book, and the staff was immensely helpful. I would especially like to thank John Gould and Cheryl Thompson of Dawson for reading the book in manuscript form. Other invaluable sources include the following published works: *Klondike* and *The Klondike Quest* by Pierre Berton, *Klondike Diary* by Robert B. Medill, *Big Pan-Out* by Kathryn Winslow, *One Man's Gold Rush* by Murray Morgan, *Women of the Klondike* by Frances Backhouse and *Alaska and the Klondike Gold Fields* by A.C. Harris.

Amongst the unpublished sources, I gained both inspiration and information from the letters or diaries of many stampeders, particularly those of Amos Lee, Georgia White, H.H. Scott and seventeen-year-old Charles P. Mosier.

Although the characters in *Destination Gold!* are fictional, their adventures and aspirations could have been shared by any number of the stampeders who traveled to the Klondike. Ned's experience with his gold claim is loosely based on that of Charley Anderson, a Swede who was tricked into buying an untried claim which later proved to be worth millions. The "Soapy" Smith mentioned in the story was a real person — Jefferson

Randolph Smith. He and his gang operated out of Skagway and were notorious for preying upon unsuspecting cheechakos.

In the writing of this book, every effort was made to ensure historical accuracy. If any errors have been made, they are my fault entirely.

I owe a debt of thanks to my publisher and editor, Bob Tyrrell, whose enthusiasm for this book — and for its subject — sustained me throughout the revising and polishing stages. Thanks also to Pierre Berton, the Klondike Visitors Association and the Yukon Arts Council for their various roles in making the Berton House Writer's Retreat a reality, and thereby giving cheechakos from Outside an opportunity to experience the North. And, finally, thanks to Patrick for his support and encouragement — and for being there to share the northern lights.

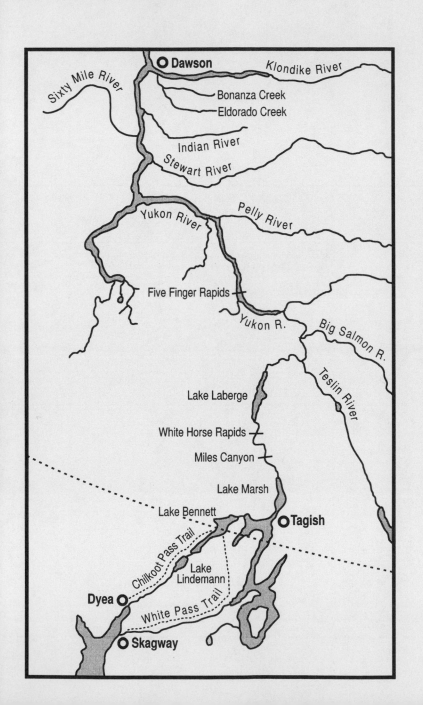

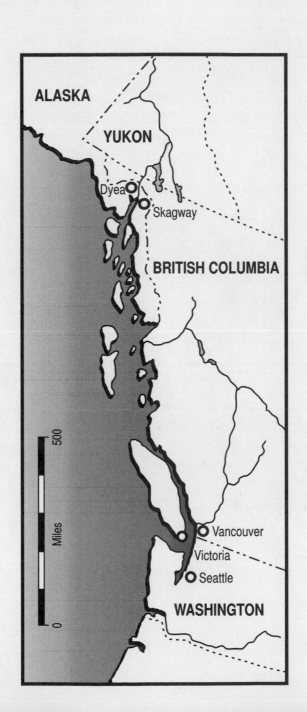

SUMMER, 1897

. 1 .

Off to the Klondike!

Victoria, BC
July 27, 1897

*I'm off to the Klondike! This morning I said my good-byes
to Mother and Sarah and boarded a steamship bound for the
North.*

*The journey of a lifetime! And the chance to make my
fortune ...*

From the diary of Ned Turner

On the morning of July 27, 1897, an enthusiastic crowd
was gathering on the wharf in Victoria, British Columbia.
Earlier that month, two boatloads of gold-laden prospectors had landed in San Francisco and Seattle with the
news of a fabulous gold discovery in the far north. From

that moment on, gold fever had taken hold and spread like a disease. The whole continent was affected. The whole world! And wherever the clamor was heard, gold-seekers by the thousands were packing their bags and heading north. The Klondike stampede was on.

Amongst the hundreds of stampeders about to set off that day, no one was more excited than Ned Turner. And no one, not even his mother, was more tearful than his twelve-year-old sister, Sarah.

"Cheer up, Sarah!" he said. "I'll be back in a tick and a promise. You know what they say — a quick trip by boat, then it's over a trail and down a river and off to the goldfields. I'll stake my claim and be home so fast you won't even know I've been gone."

"But it's so far!" Sarah wailed. "And what if, what if —"

"Oh, stop your sniveling, Sarah! You're only making it worse." Her mother handed her a dry handkerchief, then turned her attention to Ned. "Are you sure you've got everything? Food, bedding — you didn't forget your quilt, did you? And the shortbread?"

Ned began to do a mental check, his mind flitting from one category to another. Three suits of knit under-wear, six pairs of wool socks, two pairs of blanket-lined mittens ... Tin cups, granite kettle, ten pounds of soap, heavy duck sleeping bag lined with lamb's wool ... A five-foot whipsaw, ten pounds of pitch, one drifting pick and handle, one gold pan ... Ten pounds evaporated pota-toes, twenty pounds coffee, one pound mustard ... The list was endless! Enough supplies for a whole year, but he was certain he had it all.

He gave his mother an affectionate hug. "Stop worrying! See, there's my whole outfit, stacked up like a sentry with all the others. They're starting to load them now."

He'd no sooner spoken than the ship's crew began to shout. "Hoist 'er up, there! Steady, steady — Whoa! Swing 'er over more, more to the left! That's it, let 'er go!" They loaded each outfit into a net, hoisted it into the air with a large crane and swung it over a hatch in the deck. "All set with another one? Hang on! That's got it!"

Sarah winced each time someone's outfit went crashing into the hold. "How will they get it all on? There must be thousands of pounds to load up, and the boat doesn't look anywhere near that strong. And how will they get everything out? How will you ever find your own outfit, Ned? Those boxes and crates, they all look the same. And the steamboat that just docked — are you sure your gear's getting put on the right boat? You better check your ticket. Go on, Ned, check it!"

"Enough, girl!" Mother sighed with exasperation. "Ned, dear, best you go and board before our worrywart here has a fit of hysterics."

"Good-bye, then, Mother. And you, little sister. Silly goose, of course I've got the right boat. That other one's still unloading. It won't be heading north till tomorrow." He held out his arms and embraced Sarah warmly. "Everything will be fine. I'll post a letter as soon as we land, so you'll know I didn't get shipwrecked. And after that, I'll write regular. You just take care of yourself. Promise?"

Sarah gave a loud sniff and nodded tearfully.

"Well ... That's it, then." Ned smiled and gave his

mother one last hug. Then he pushed his way through the jostling crowd, strode up the gangplank, and on to the upper deck.

He leaned over the rail and waved vigorously as the boat steamed out of the harbor. He could see that his mother was crying as hard as Sarah, now that he was truly on his way. But Ned knew she had no second thoughts. "It's the chance of a lifetime," she'd said when they first heard the news about the Klondike. She hadn't needed to add that it was also a chance to pay off Father's debts.

Ned knew that his father's death two years earlier had left unexpected debts that would take years to pay off without a windfall of some sort, even with Ned quitting school and going to work. And here it was. The Klondike gold rush, a windfall for the world.

The steamboat was packed with men all thinking the same. They were a lively bunch, all ages, from all walks of life, exuberant and full of optimism. At sixteen, Ned was the youngest, but he looked the part of the prospector, dressed like the others in his brand new Klondike garb. As the city faded from view, he straightened his hat proudly and yelled, "Good-bye, Victoria! See you when I'm rich!"

"Rich, is it?" A large, bushy-haired man standing at the rail turned to Ned with a grin. "You and how many others?"

"All of us!" Ned exclaimed. "There's gold for the picking up there. Didn't you read about those prospectors? They all struck it rich! One of them found gold right under a boulder, over eight hundred dollars' worth of nuggets. There's tons of gold up there, that's what the newspapers say. Isn't that why you're going?" He glanced at the diamond ring sparkling on the man's finger. "Maybe you're rich enough already."

"You can never be too rich, kid!" The man extended a hand. "Montana's the name, though I'm most recently from Seattle. Montana Jim Daley, if you want the whole moniker, but folks just call me Montana."

"Pleased to meet you," Ned said. "I'm Edward Turner, but everyone calls me Ned."

"Anything you need, you come to me."

"Thank you, sir. That's very kind."

"Sir, is it? My, oh my. From England, are you? Buckingham Palace? Your accent sounds mighty princely."

Ned laughed. "My parents came from England, but I was born in Victoria. And my house is hardly Buckingham Palace."

"Well, you come see me if you need anything. I mean it, now. I can see you're on your own. Never been away from home, have you? A word of advice, Sir Buckingham. Don't be too trusting. Everyone's after the same thing and there's only so much to go around. In spite of what you hear."

Ned nodded as the older man continued to give advice. He'd be careful, all right. And he'd definitely consider Montana a friend.

. 2 .

Catherine

Not everyone on Victoria's harbor that July morning was excited by the prospect of gold. Catherine wasn't. The slight, dark-haired girl had disembarked from a northbound steamer with only one thought in her mind. And it wasn't a stack of bright yellow metal.

It wasn't that she was unaware of the gold rush. She'd been one of the first to see the now famous *Portland* steaming into Seattle the morning of July the seventeenth. She'd even seen the passengers filing off, staggering under the weight of their now famous baggage.

She hadn't planned it that way. She'd been paddling all night, and it was pure coincidence that she'd arrived at the wharf the same time as the steamer. And on the morning of her sixteenth birthday.

It was dawn when she'd come in sight of the city, and to her astonishment, she'd found the dock swarming with people. Her initial feeling was panic. Had the police found out already? Was the crowd waiting for her?

When a boisterous cheer indicated that the crowd's attention was fixed on a small steamboat puffing into the dock, Catherine's panic gave way to relief. With so much excitement, no one would notice her.

She reached the shore and pushed her canoe back out to sea. By the time she'd climbed up to the wharf, the steamboat passengers were already coming down the gangplank. It crossed Catherine's mind what a ragged lot they were, and how unusual their baggage was. They weren't carrying valises or carpet bags, but an odd assortment of moosehide sacks, bits of canvas and rolled-up blankets. Still, it had nothing to do with her.

As she pressed on, she noticed that on every corner, on every street, all the way to the railroad station, the clamor was the same. Gold! Gold! Go North! Go North! Even before Catherine boarded her train, the newsboys were brandishing the headlines — 68 RICH MEN ON THE STEAMER PORTLAND! STACKS OF YELLOW METAL!

It was of no interest to Catherine. She got on the train for San Francisco and waited nervously for its departure. When the whistle screeched, when steam billowed from the engine, when the wheels rumbled out of the city, only then did she unclench her fists and breathe more easily. And when the train picked up speed and began to roar through the countryside, only then did she allow herself one small moment of exhilaration. She'd done it!

Gone the city, gone the island, gone the life ... The words echoed the rhythm of the wheels as the train rolled south. By the end of the day, someone would discover what Catherine had left behind. But by then, she, too, would be gone.

She hadn't planned to leave San Francisco after a mere four days. But in the overall scheme of things, her plans had never been of much consequence. So here she was in Victoria, with only one thought in mind: Escape.

Exactly what she was escaping was not apparent to anyone who happened to notice her. Not that anyone did. Throngs of people continued to wave as the north-bound ship steamed out of the Inner Harbour. Many onlookers stared longingly at the steamboat, no doubt wondering how they could scrape together enough money to buy a stampeder's outfit. Peddlers who hadn't managed to sell their dogs and horses to the outgoing batch of stampeders continued to wend their way through the crowd, hoping to find buyers amongst the next batch.

Catherine paid no attention as she hurried across the wharf and along the busy street. Only a close inspection would reveal a wariness in her eyes, a hint of fear. She kept telling herself there was no need to be afraid. She was safe in Victoria. She was in a different country, far from the nightmare that had forced her from the island. She was a different person altogether, a far cry from the girl who'd fled in the dark a thousand lifetimes ago.

Even so, the sight of two constables on the corner made her falter. She turned away quickly, afraid they might recognize her face. But they didn't seem to notice.

She moved on, reassured that no one would know who she was. Or where she came from. Or what she'd done.

On the other hand ... She caught sight of her reflection in a storefront window and grimaced. If anyone gave her half a glance, they would see that she'd been hurt. Her unruly hair, falling in tangled clumps over her face, couldn't quite hide the gash on her right temple, nor the bruise that swelled like an over-ripe peach across her eyes and down her cheek. If anyone asked, she'd tell them she'd walked into a door. No one needed to know the truth.

Farther down the street, the crowd was thinning out. People started to notice her. Catherine could tell by the sniffs and looks of disapproval they didn't much like her wild appearance. So be it. She had learned from an early age not to care.

What she needed was a cheap hotel or some sort of rooming house, a place where she could catch her breath, rest for a bit, get used to the feel of solid ground. She needed to clean herself up, too. Six days on an over-crowded steamer hadn't helped her appearance. A proper wash, a thorough combing-out of her hair — that would have to do. She'd left in too much of a hurry to pack a change of clothes, and she didn't have enough money to buy new ones. As for her face ... Time would take care of the cut and the bruise. And time would take care of the nightmare.

She set her mouth in a determined line and marched into the first likely-looking hotel she came to. Three nights, that would do it. Then she would look for a job. And begin a new life altogether.

. 3 .

A Bit of Bad Luck

Early August, 1897

*We've almost reached Skagway, after seven days on the
water. The scenery was grand. Mountains, porpoises, whales
and sunshine! Many of my fellow passengers were green
around the gills, but I fared none too badly. Nor did my
new friend Montana.*

No sooner had the ship dropped anchor than Ned began
to think Sarah was right. He'd never find his own gear. He
watched in horror as the stampeders' outfits were removed
from the hold, hurled on to waiting scows, then dumped
haphazardly on to the beach. By the time he reached shore,
his carefully packed belongings were mixed up with everyone else's. Hundreds of outfits were watersoaked, many
had burst open, and all around him a desperate horde
cursed and argued and fought over whose gear was whose

and which outfit was which. And finding one's gear was only the first part. They then had to move it above the high-water mark to beat the incoming tide.

In the midst of the frantic mob, only Montana appeared calm. "Slow down, Buckingham," he said as Ned struggled up the beach with his fifth load. "You'll wear yourself out before you even start." He stroked his beard thoughtfully. "I been thinking. How about we go in together? There'll be snow on the pass before long, but I see you got a sled, and I got a good strong horse. We can pack our outfits with no trouble at all. Whaddya say, partner?"

"Sure!" Ned smiled, pleased at this unexpected bit of luck. "Where did you get the horse? He wasn't on the ship coming up, was he?"

Montana winked. "Won 'im in a card game on board. I'll be picking 'im up in Skagway. Listen, I staked out a camping spot near the start of the trail. Real good position, and you're welcome to share it. How about I haul up the rest of your gear while you pitch your tent and start a fire? Is it a deal?"

"You bet! But where's your outfit? Hadn't you better bring it up before the tide comes in?"

Montana tapped the side of his head. "Always thinking, Buckingham. I aim to buy my outfit in Skagway. Couldn't see the sense of dragging it up the beach. But enough of this jabbering. We better get a move on. That tide's creeping up fast."

Once all the gear was moved and Ned's camp was set up, they shared some beans cooked over the fire. Ned was looking forward to a good sleep on solid ground when Montana said, "You up for a few hands of poker? Last chance before we hit the trail. Maybe you could win us another horse."

"I'm not sure ..."

"Ah, c'mon. Do you good to have a bit of relaxation. It's gonna be a rough road over the next few weeks. Besides, this infernal midnight sun — well, you can see for yourself it's goin' on ten at night and still as bright as day. You ain't gonna be able to sleep. And you gotta see Skagway. They got everything, even a telegraph office. Say, you could send a message to your ma! She'd have it by the end of the week."

With that, Ned was persuaded.

• • •

Skagway was a ramshackle tent town, bursting with men having one last card game or shot of whiskey before they tackled the White Pass Trail. A fellow could buy a haircut, have his laundry done, pay for a bath or buy a meal in a tattered tent-restaurant — at highly inflated prices.

Ned was shocked. "Beans and bacon for $2.50? That'd only cost a quarter in Victoria!" Good thing he'd already bought the recommended one hundred pounds of beans and two hundred pounds of bacon.

The telegraph office was no better. "One whole dollar to send a telegram? That's outrageous!"

"Sure, it'll cost you a dollar," Montana said. "But think how quick it'll get there. Your ma'll sleep easy, knowing you got here safe. And ain't that worth a dollar or two?"

"It's worth every penny," Ned agreed. He sent the telegram, thinking how happy his mother and Sarah would be to hear that he'd arrived safely, and with all his goods intact.

There was another side to Skagway. Everywhere Ned looked, he saw horses — shoeless, starving, bleeding from pack sores, half-dead and swarming with flies. The carcasses of those that had already died were left to rot in the streets.

The stench made Ned's stomach reel and the sight sickened his heart. "How can people treat them like that? It's not humane! It's ... it's barbaric!"

Montana merely laughed. "Kid, you're some cheechako. You think they'd've been turned loose if there was any more work in 'em? Those beasts have earned their keep and there's an end to it. If you feel that sorry, you go ahead 'n' pay two hundred bucks for a ton o' hay."

"Two hundred?" Ned was aghast. "What about your horse? Can you afford to feed him?"

"Don't you worry none about that."

"And the dogs!" Ned went on. "I just — Oh, it's criminal." Every few steps they were forced to dodge a starving mutt, abandoned because the poor thing had turned out to be useless in a harness. There were dozens of dogs for sale, too, at one hundred dollars apiece. But it was obvious not all were cut out to be sled dogs.

One lanky mutt, a German shepherd cross, reminded Ned of the dog he and Sarah once had, except for the torn ear and broken tooth. "Where'd you come from, eh, fella?" he said when the dog came and sniffed his hand. He gave him a pat and a scratch behind the ear.

"Don't encourage it!" Montana waved a fist in a threatening way. "Get outa here, mangy mutt!"

The dog shied away.

"'Prob'ly somebody's pet," Montana said. "They get kidnapped down south and brought up here. Useless things. But there's more 'n' enough fools that'll buy 'em."

"Something should be done about it," Ned said. "It's not right."

He was so preoccupied with the state of dogs and horses, he was scarcely aware that Montana had steered him into a large white tent. There was no question it was a gambling tent and, judging by the crowd, one of the most popular places in town. Crates had been set up as tables, and at every table men sat elbow to elbow, slapping down their cards. Others jostled at the makeshift bar in the corner, and still more squeezed in behind the players, waiting for a turn.

One group spotted Montana and called him over. "Here we go," Montana said, taking Ned by the arm. "Looks like they saved us a place."

"Wait, I don't think ..."

"Shucks, kid! You're off on a man's adventure, aren't you? Play a hand or two! Be a man!"

"Well, since you put it that way ..." Ned blushed self-consciously but raised his head a little higher. He joined the others and soon found himself being dealt in for a game of poker.

It didn't take him long to learn the rules, and much to

his surprise, he won. To celebrate, Montana bought him a whiskey. "Bottom's up, kid."

"Thanks!" Ned took a drink, then gasped and sputtered as the burning liquid hit the back of his throat.

"Your first, I take it," Montana said. The others laughed.

Ned pushed the glass aside and ordered a lemonade. He'd have to keep his wits about him if he was going to win the next hand.

But he lost the next hand, and the two that followed. Lost not only his winnings, but virtually all of his money. "I don't believe it," he moaned. "How could I? All right, then. One more game. This'll be the lucky one." It had to be. He'd lost all his money and now owed even more. One of the players told him not to worry. They wouldn't press him to pay it back. If he lost again, they'd take it in kind. Whatever that meant.

His head was too fuzzy to think it through. Besides, the cards were already in his hand. He stared at them, confused. Hearts blended into diamonds. Black spots blurred into shapes he could hardly recognize. A king leered mockingly.

He blinked and tried to focus. The tent was stifling. The ground seemed to roll like swells on the sea. Nine, ace, six ... what was he supposed to do? Pick up, discard ...

Before he knew it, the game was over and a pox-scarred man called Rooster was grinning across the table. "Whaddya know, kid? Looks like I won your outfit."

"No!" Ned was stunned. He hadn't bet his entire outfit, had he? Mother had mortgaged their house to buy his outfit. And to throw it away on a game of cards? He couldn't have!

He wiped his sweating forehead. He had to get outside, away from the reek of cigar smoke and whiskey, away from the swirling walls of the tent. He stood up and stumbled from the table.

"Here, kid, lemme help."

"Leave me alone!" He pushed Montana aside and staggered out of the tent. Heedless of the crowd, he sank to the ground, buried his face in his hands and cried, "How could I! How could I be so stupid!" He should've walked away from the tent, right from the beginning. But oh, no, Montana's comment about being a man ... That's what did it. Feeling grown up and proud of it.

What would Father have said? Ned could imagine the disapproving tone and the words — *pride cometh before a fall*. Well. Ned now knew the feeling.

A few moments later Montana appeared. He crouched beside Ned and patted his shoulder. "Don't take it so hard, Buckingham. I'll get your outfit back."

"How? I've only got one dollar left to pay you. I lost everything!"

"Look. Soapy Smith, the fella that runs that gambling tent, he's an ol' pal of mine. I'll see what I can do."

"If you could ..." Ned felt a glimmer of hope. "Oh, gosh, if there's anything — I'll pay you back, I promise. As soon as I stake my claim."

"We'll work it out. Meanwhile, you go on back to the camp, try 'n' get some shut-eye. You're tuckered out and no wonder. So, whaddya say? Sound like a plan?"

Ned nodded gratefully. Any plan would do. He had nothing left to lose.

• • •

Back at the camp, Ned saw that most of his belongings were gone. All that remained was the tent, his sleeping bag and one grub box. Rooster had clearly wasted no time carting away his winnings. As if he knew all along, Ned thought bitterly. As if he had a wagon all ready and waiting.

As he stared at the empty camp, trying to figure out where he'd gone wrong, a whimpering sound caught his attention. He turned around, and there was the fur-matted wreck of a dog.

"I know how you feel," Ned said, holding out a hand. "I feel abandoned, too."

The dog approached cautiously, sniffed Ned's hand, then licked his fingers. His tail wagged as Ned reached into his grub box and tore off a chunk of stale bread. "Here you go, boy. But that's all you get."

The dog gulped down the bread, gave Ned's fingers another lick and scuttled away.

A short time later, Ned was wakened by the sound of a horse and wagon pulling up to the tent. "Hey, Buckingham!" a voice called out. "Get your hide out here. Today's your lucky day."

When Ned went outside, he saw a wagon overloaded with goods, including the sacks and crates of his own outfit. His face cracked in a smile. "You got it back!"

"Just like I promised," Montana said. "Got my own outfit at the same time, so we're all set. And this here's the horse. Darn sight better 'n' most, wouldn't you say?"

Ned could hardly speak. "Gosh, Montana, I don't know —" His voice broke with emotion.

"You don't know how to thank me. I know, I'm one heck of a guy. But don't you go gettin' all soft on me. I'll make sure you pay me back."

"Good," Ned said, as firmly as he could manage. "I owe you so much. Don't worry, I won't let you down."

Later, when he was checking through his supplies, Ned discovered that his whole outfit hadn't been returned. All the extras were gone, the special treats his mother had packed. A round of cheese, a can of maple syrup, a tin of Mother's shortbread, a jar of the homemade bread-and-butter pickles he loved. His quilt was gone, too. Worst of all, he was missing his Bible, the last gift he'd ever received from his father.

An ache welled up inside. The loss of these few precious items was almost too great to bear. But he couldn't bring himself to say anything, not when Montana had been so kind.

• • •

"Wake up, Sir Buckingham!"

The voice startled Ned out of a deep sleep, and for a moment he wasn't sure where he was. Then he remembered, and his depression of the previous night gave way to renewed excitement. The White Pass Trail! Today was the day the journey would really begin.

"Coffee's hot," Montana said. "And you better get some grub in your belly. It's gonna be a long day."

It was five o'clock in the morning and already full light. Not a moment to lose! Ned splashed cold water on his face and threw together some breakfast. He had almost finished eating when he saw the dog poking his head around the side of the tent. He spooned some beans and bacon on to a chunk of bread and held it out. "Here, boy. C'mon."

The dog gulped it down and wagged his tail. Afterwards, as Ned was loading up, he stuck to Ned's side like a barnacle on a rock.

Montana wasn't impressed. "Whaddya think you're doing? We're not taking that mutt. Go on, git!" He picked up a rock and hurled it, hitting the dog square in the rump. The dog yelped and ran off, but in no time at all he was back.

"Nugget, that's what I'll call him," Ned said. "He'll help carry my load and bring us good luck. Won't you, boy?"

The dog barked excitedly.

"Nugget," Montana scoffed. "You're a coupla nuggets short of a poke, kid. But have it your way. And don't say I never warned you. At least the horse is gonna earn its keep." He strapped a packsaddle on to his horse and loaded it sky-high.

"Come on, Nugget," Ned said. "We'll show him. Let's see what you can carry." He slung a small canvas saddle-bag across Nugget's back, filled it with a light load and thanked his stars the dog didn't shy away.

That done, he hoisted his eighty-pound pack and set off at an energetic pace. That bit of bad luck in Skagway, that was over and done with. From now on things would be better. Life was grand! He was young and strong and determined. He had his gear back, a dog that was pulling his weight, a knowledgeable companion and, best of all, the promise of gold at the end of the trail.

. 4 .

A Change of Plans

Catherine hadn't planned to come to Victoria. But for someone who'd never had much success with plans, she had to admit she was doing rather well.

That hadn't been the case in San Francisco. She had gone there hoping to find her mother. For three days she'd searched, wandering through vaguely remembered streets, knocking on the doors of derelict hotels and rooming houses. She'd finally tracked down a few of her mother's friends, the ones she remembered from childhood. Your mother's gone, some told her. Others said bluntly, She drank herself to death.

Catherine had felt an unexpected sense of loss. Unexpected, because she'd never really known her mother. She'd abandoned Catherine when she was six years old, shortly after they'd moved to Seattle.

As for Catherine's father ... She'd learned that he'd moved back to San Francisco the previous year but had died a few months later. Shot down in an alley, her source told her. Owed a lot of people a lot of money.

Catherine was sorry. Not that he was dead. But that someone hadn't killed him sooner.

The news about her parents gave her a tremendous sense of freedom. Now everyone from her past was gone. For the first time in her life she could make her own choices.

She was determined to choose wisely. She wouldn't hurry, she'd take her time. She certainly wouldn't draw attention to herself. Not until she was certain she was out of danger.

One day, as she was walking near the San Francisco harbor, trying to decide what her next step might be, she saw an ad in the window of a steamship office.

Tickets to Skagway, Gateway to the Klondike!
Overnight stop in Victoria!

Catherine had no intention of going north to the Klondike. But why not Victoria? A new place, free of memories and associations ... Right then and there she had booked her passage, and left the following day.

Once she'd settled in Victoria, it hadn't taken long to find a job. Gold-rush fever, as frenzied in Victoria as it was in San Francisco and Seattle, was sweeping away workers by the hundreds. Nearly every shop Catherine passed had a Help Wanted sign in its window.

A sign in a tailor's shop seemed the most promising.

Wanted Immediately. Fair Hand with a Needle.

Summoning up the courage for an interview, Catherine stepped inside.

"Walked into a door, did you?"

The tailor's unexpected greeting caught Catherine off guard, and for a moment she wasn't sure what he meant. Then she saw where he was staring, and her hand flew up to cover her bruised face. "Y-yes," she stammered. Her cheeks grew hot. *What must he be thinking? That I'm clumsy and awkward and can't see straight? Some fair hand I'd be. How can I stitch a seam if I can't see a door?* The interview was finished. "I-I'm sorry to trouble you," she said, and turned to leave.

"The job's yours if you want it."

"Wh-what?"

"You heard me. And if you're willing to work extra hours, you can live in the room upstairs. That bruise of yours ... I know how it is." He gave her a sympathetic smile.

Catherine started that very day. The tailor, Mr. Pendygrasse, gave her a quick lesson on the sewing machine, set her up with needles and bobbins and thread, and handed her a stack of shirt pieces to stitch. Then he left her alone, without asking one single question.

As the weeks went by, Catherine felt increasingly safe in Victoria. She could've been happy. If it weren't for the nightmare.

It was always the same ...

A young girl with dark hair and brown eyes sits on a ramshackle porch. Someone has given her a peach. It's a treat, and she's eating it slowly. Warm, juicy and sweet, the taste of summer. She hears voices inside the shack, bottles clinking, the snap-rustle-snap of cards. Then one husky voice, louder than the rest, shouts, "She's worth her weight in gold!" Another laughs, "So take her. She's all yours."

The dream shifts to an island. She hears the same husky voice. "You think you got nine lives? I'll give you one less." Eight of spades, seven diamonds, six of clubs. No queen. No hearts.

She hears muffled blows in the night. Five of clubs. Four of clubs. Blows falling, falling, fall ... Winter ... The dark cedar walls close in. There's no escape from the island.

The dream shifts again. To another summer. Another night. Only this time the girl strikes a blow. Hears the crack on bone, and strikes again. I'll take your nine lives! Three of clubs, then two and, at last, the ace. A full house.

With the final blow she's caught. She struggles help-lessly, swearing she hadn't meant to do it, she's done nothing wrong, she's worth her weight in gold. But he drags her to the water. Strands of seaweed tighten around her throat ...

Whenever she had the nightmare, Catherine woke up feeling drenched. Not from the still sea water, but from the pool of blood on the floor.

. 5 .

The White Pass Trail

Late August, 1897

*Almost finished hauling through the Canyon. Then we'll set up
a new base camp at Porcupine Hill. The trail is a nightmare,
worse than I could have imagined. I heard it was comparatively
easy. Compared to what? I should have taken the Chilkoot
route, but no use crying over spilt milk. The weather has turned
rainy and foul. A person can't stop to think, let alone to rest.
And the horses ... Better not think about the horses.*

"Get up there, you useless sack o' bones! Move, blast you,
move!"

Ned shuddered as Montana's whip bit into the side
of his horse. The poor creature was already suffering from
sores on his back, and his hoofs were bleeding from the
sharp rocks of the trail. He reared and neighed, his eyes
huge with fright.

Doubled over with his own heavy pack, Ned could stand it no longer. "Stop hitting him!" he shouted. "He's overloaded, you can see he's losing his balance! Give me the rope!"

"There's no time!" Montana pushed Ned against the rocks and continued to beat the animal. "You scurvy beast, you'll move if it kills you!" Then he turned on Ned. "And if you can't get that dog moving, I will!"

Ned set his jaw, gave Nugget a gentle nudge and grimly moved on.

For days they'd been climbing through ankle-deep rivers of mud, past sinkholes that sucked in packs and horses and dogs alike. They'd struggled over paths strewn with jagged rocks and boulders and fallen trees, then fought their way along precipices where one careless step meant a five-hundred-foot drop to certain death.

Ned's feet no longer felt like his. The thin soles of his gumboots made every bone as sore as a boil. The skin was raw and blistered from the water sloshing inside his boots. Every ligament was sprained from slipping and climbing over the rocks.

As for the trail! Slick with slime, churned up by hundreds of tramping feet and barely wide enough for a horse, it twisted in hairpin curves toward the summit.

And if the smell of rotting horse flesh was bad in Skagway, it was ten thousand times worse on the trail. The stench arising from the riverbank painted a grisly picture of what lay below.

Day after day they wallowed in water and mud. They worked wet and slept wet. There was never any heat in the tent. The little folding grate Ned had bought to go over the fire was light to carry and useful as a stove, but as a source of heat it was useless. Nothing got dry.

It will never end, Ned thought as he moved the last of his gear to the top of Porcupine Hill. There'd be more rain and thousands more feet to churn up the gumbo. The trail would soon be impassable. Then what? Not a chance of getting through till winter set in and froze the whole sickening mess. But that could be two months away.

Finally he reached the site for their next base camp. He could scarcely move for the pain in his feet and legs and shoulders and back, but there was still more work to be done.

He removed Nugget's saddlebag and set up the tent. Once that was done, he lit a fire, placed the grate over top and heated some beans. Montana, meanwhile, leaned against a log to enjoy his chewing tobacco.

"Aren't you going to unload the horse?" Ned asked. "He's exhausted! And shouldn't you feed him?"

"With what, Buckingham? I already told you what hay cost. You got that kind o' money for a horse?"

"But he's hungry!"

"Hungry? Sure he's hungry. And unless you packed the hay, he's gonna stay hungry. Same as that scrawny mutt you insisted on bringing. What're you planning to feed it?"

"Some of my food, same as I've been doing all along. Don't worry, it's from my grub box, not yours." To prove his point, Ned emptied the partially cooked beans on to his plate, ate half, then passed the remainder to the dog. "Here you go, Nugget," he said. The dog attacked it greedily.

Montana shook his head. "A piece of advice, Bucking-ham. I'm thinking your heart's too soft for the Klondike. I'm thinking you'd be better off turning back and taking the first boat home."

"I'm not turning back!" Ned flushed with indigna-tion. Who did Montana think he was, criticizing Ned just because he wanted to feed his dog? He'd show him. If making it to the Klondike meant you had to be hard-hearted, then he'd be hard-hearted. He snatched the plate away from Nugget and snapped, "Beat it!" Then he gave the dog a kick.

The startled dog yelped and slunk a few feet away.

Ned stared into the fire, his whole body shaking. He listened to the sputter and hiss of falling rain, filled with self-loathing, and wondered what kind of person he was turning out to be.

•   •   •

The worst part of the trail was not that the stampeders had to get over it, but that they had to get over it several times. They moved in five-mile stages, packing sixty- to eighty-pound loads to the next staging point. There they cached their goods and returned for more.

Ned's mackinaw was splattered with mud and torn ragged from the sharp rocks on the trail. His boots gave him such terrible blisters he wanted to cry out at every step. Still he pressed on, mentally whipping himself as brutally as Montana whipped the horse.

As they climbed to the summit, snow began to fall. It continued to fall. And day after day, no matter how steadily it piled up, each new fall of snow was packed down, hard as concrete, by the thousands of feet tramping over the trail.

The line of men was so long and tightly packed there was never a break. Men who collapsed at the side of the trail because of illness or exhaustion begged to be let back in line. But no one would stop.

Ned felt dehumanized, a mere link in a continuous chain of struggling humans and straining animals. His only thought was to get to the summit.

He drowned out the sounds around him. The gasps, the curses, the groans of men. The screams of the animals.

He himself had become a pack animal. He carried sixty pounds on his back and another fifty on the sled he'd harnessed himself to. His heart pounded with the strain. His lungs felt fit to burst.

How long ago was it that Montana's horse had collapsed? The heavy load and beatings had taken their toll. When the horse finally stopped and sunk to its knees, unable to take another step, the enraged Montana had broken his whip across its flanks. Then he'd unloaded the gear and left the horse lying on the trail.

When Ned looked back a few moments later, the horse was gone. The crush of men pressing up from behind had trodden it into the snow.

Nugget gamely plodded on. He was now pulling a sled as well as carrying a twenty-pound pack. Ned refused to load him more heavily. In spite of his determination to be hard-hearted, he couldn't help but care for the dog. Whenever Nugget halted on the trail and raised a paw, Ned removed the pellets of ice that had formed between his toes. And every few steps the dog stopped and looked around as if to make sure Ned was following.

Yes, I'm still here, Ned wanted to say. I haven't turned tail yet. You and me, we're not giving up.

He couldn't say the words out loud. He didn't have the strength. Instead he gave the dog what was probably more of a grimace than a smile, and staggered on.

• • •

By the end of August they were almost over the pass. They had set up a camping place at the summit, and once their final load was transported, they could begin the descent.

Things are bound to improve, Ned thought hopefully. If it weren't for Montana being such a thorn in the side. And if weren't for the stormy weather ...

He lay in his sleeping bag and prayed for sleep. His clothing, soaked through from sweat and snow, was frozen to his body. He couldn't stop shaking.

As the blizzard howled outside the tent, his fears jostled in his mind. Everything will be covered with snow. The cache we left down the trail, our one last load, will we be able to find it, buried with so many others? Did I remember to leave a marker?

He tossed and turned in the cold sleeping bag, worrying endlessly. Sometimes he heard his sister's voice, wailing along with the wind. What if you can't see your way clear to go down? What if you're lost and buried? What if ... What if ... And his mother's blustery voice, snapping in impatient gusts, You worrywart, Ned! You're having a fit of hysterics! Stop it, stop it, stop it!

Finally he fell into a fretful sleep.

He dreamed the blizzard was a ghostly presence that mocked his foolhardy adventure. You'll never make it, the blizzard laughed. You're not a man, you're just a kid. You'll never make it over the pass ...

He waved the blizzard aside and slid down the trail, straight to the mound of snow that covered his gear. Frantically he began to dig it out, while fighting off the desperate men who claimed it didn't belong to him. No matter how hard he tried, he couldn't fight them off. There were too many. They were too strong. They tore his belongings apart with their bare hands.

Then Ned realized the men were right. It wasn't his gear. But why were his things scattered about? His Bible, his quilt, the shortbread — everything he'd lost had been found. He had to hurry. Hurry down the mountain, hurry to stop the blizzard, hurry to grab hold of his Bible —

Too late. The wind ripped the pages. Bits of white paper fluttered over the pass like snowflakes.

Hurry, Ned! someone called out. Was it Sarah? Or Mother?

No, it was Father. Hurry, Ned! See the page with the inscription? *From your loving father.* Don't let it go! Hurry before it's lost!

Ned reached out in panic. But instead of grasping

hold of the precious scrap of paper, his hand plunged into a mess of maggots, squirming into the flanks of a dead and rotting horse.

He woke up screaming. The trail, the horrors — he couldn't go on. But he couldn't go back. He was doomed to stay, tormented with cold and despair.

Just then, a small movement caught his eye. Nugget was crawling under the tent flap. With a whimper, the dog laid his head on Ned's chest. They spent the rest of the night curled up together, keeping each other warm.

By morning, Ned had forgotten his nightmare. He got up, ate the usual cold beans and flapjacks, and set out almost eagerly, anxious to reach his last load. "Come on, Nugget," he said. "One last run. Then we can say we made it over the White Pass."

A short time later, Montana caught up to Ned on the trail and gave him an amused look. "What's got into you this morning? You sound like a flippin' chickadee."

"The worst is over!" Ned grinned. "One more load and we can take off to Lake Bennett. Weather there's milder, everyone says so."

Montana grunted. "Reckon everyone said the White Pass Trail was a pleasant stroll. Reckon nobody knows a darn fool thing."

"Well, there's one thing I know," Ned declared. "That mound of snow over there is covering our loads. I was worried last night, thought I'd forgotten to mark it. But see the tip of the pick sticking out? That's the marker. I put it there myself."

"Good for you!" Montana dug out the gear and began loading it on to the sled while Ned adjusted Nugget's harness. When he stepped back and saw what Montana had put on the sled, he was horrified. "That's over fifty pounds! Nugget can't pull that! I'm carrying one of those packs and so are you."

"Says who? I'm done with packing while this mutt does next to nothing. See them other dogs? They're pulling two hundred pounds. And this useless —"

"He's been pulling and carrying heavy loads and you know it!" Ned retorted. "If you hadn't beaten that poor horse to death!"

Montana snorted with contempt. "You never give up, do you? A regular pit bull, that's what you are. Come on, get moving!" He aimed a kick at the dog.

Nugget strained to move forward, but not only was the load too heavy, the snow was sticking to the sled's iron runners.

Meanwhile, the line of men stretching behind was growing restless. "Get movin' up there!" someone yelled. Other voices joined in.

"Move!" Montana hollered at the dog.

Ned knocked a load off the sled and hoisted it on to his own back. He'd carry double if he had to. "Come on, there's a good dog," he said, pulling on the harness. "You can do it."

Montana pushed from behind and the sled started to move.

"Last load, boy," Ned kept saying. "You can do it." He hoped he could do the same.

He thought of his father, and how he would've fared

on the trail. Bravely, of course. Heroically. And with high spirits.

Then the truth hit him. Father would never have come in the first place. A fool's errand, he would have called it, and fought Ned every step of the way. He would have treated it as another one of Ned's hare-brained schemes, one of the many plans Ned had embarked upon, only to lose interest and give up when success wasn't quick and easy to come by. He would have refused to spend a penny on Ned's outfit. Would have seen nothing but danger and discomfort, disease, most likely, and distress. He would have said, If you go, it will break your mother's heart.

The truth was, if Father were alive it would have broken *his* heart to see Ned set out for the Klondike.

Mother, on the other hand, had given him nothing but encouragement. Ned wouldn't let her down. Nor would he let down his father. Of course there would have been a row. After all, if Father hadn't died, Ned would still have been in school. He would have quit to join the stampede. Father would have railed, When have you ever stuck to anything? You, find gold in the Klondike? You're doomed to failure!

Oh, yes, there would have been one terrific row. But once the dust had settled ...

"Hey, Buckingham, what time next year is this?" Montana, with his lighter load, was waiting as Ned stumbled to their camp at the summit. "Didn't figure you'd take so long."

Ned didn't bother answering. Once they got to Lake Bennett he'd continue on his own. Montana was more than a thorn in the side. He was a foot-long spike in the boot.

The next morning, as Ned set off on the next stage of the journey, he thought again of his father. Yes, there would've been a row. But when all was said and done, Father would have been proud to see Ned make it. To see him reach the promised land of gold.

. 6 .
Sarah

Victoria, September 15, 1897

Dear Ned,

Why don't you write? It's been almost tow whole months and we have'nt heard a word. Mother says its because you're to busy shoveling up the gold. Is that the reason? If it is pleese put the shovel down and pick up your pen. We want to hear all about your adventure. And we want to know that your all right.

I'm back at school now and I can assure you it's as dreary as ever. Mother is still taking in washing and that's very dreary also. We spend a lot of time at the church and everyone, espeshly the Waverleys, are always asking about you and the Klondike. We never know what to say.

I miss you terribly. So does Mother.

Sometimes I think that she wishes ...

Sarah paused and chewed the end of her pencil. What she was thinking could not be written in a letter, especially not in a letter her mother would insist on reading. She could hear it now. This word's misspelled, Sarah. This apostrophe's in the wrong place. This handwriting's a disgrace.

Only after the corrections had been made would Mother reread the letter for the content. And she would not be pleased to read what Sarah was really thinking. *Sometimes I think that Mother wishes I had gone north instead of you.*

Sarah had always felt closer to her father and brother, and now that she was alone with her mother, the gulf between them was wider than ever. It didn't matter whether Sarah was home or not, for all the attention Mother gave her. Unless it was to scold or criticize. Sarah was too slow, too sloppy, too careless, too moody. She was forever being told, Get your head out of the clouds! Get your feet on the ground! Get your nose out of the book! Moments before she'd started her latest letter to Ned, Mother had complained, "You'll be the death of me, young lady, if you don't stop moaning about. You've got a face like curdled milk, it's that sour."

Sarah had wanted to shout, No wonder! My father's dead, my brother's gone to the ends of the earth, and my own mother hates me!

She hadn't said anything of the sort. Instead, she'd bitten her tongue and promised to be more cheerful.

She longed to ask Ned for some advice on how to get along with their mother. He was so pleasant he could charm the sting out of a bee. Not sullen Sarah.

And if she wasn't moaning about, she was worrying. Like this morning. "Why hasn't Ned written? He must be sick. Or hurt. Did the ship even make it? There wasn't anything in the newspaper, was there, about a storm or a shipwreck? Oh, Mother! What if he drowned? What if —"

"For goodness sake, child! Stop imagining the worst! Ned's fine. He's too busy to write, that's all. Busy being active! He's a doer, Sarah, like me. You're a dreamer, just like your father. You're so much a look-before-you-leap kind of person, you never leap at all. Not that I don't love you, mind, but goodness me, you spend so much time daydreaming and what-iffing, you never get around to *doing* anything! You're just — Oh, I don't know."

You're just *dull*. Sarah knew that's what her mother meant to say. You're a dull and stodgy worrywart.

Sarah's classmates thought the same. Whenever plans were afoot for some sort of outing, they always said, Don't ask Sarah. She can never keep up. She's always complaining. She's too much of a scaredy-cat.

She'd been shocked when her mother had so heartily embraced Ned's plan to go north. When he'd quit his job — jumped right over the department store counter — and rushed off to buy a steamboat ticket, Mother hadn't worried. She hadn't fretted about the loss of wages, or about her only son going so far away. No, instead of being furious, she'd gone out and mortgaged their house. Then bought Ned not only a ten-foot stack of supplies, but a studio portrait of himself, all decked out for the Klondike.

Sarah studied the portrait, standing in its place of honor on top of the writing desk. For the millionth time she stared at her tall, handsome brother in his new mackinaw, boots and wide-brimmed hat, standing in front of the painted backdrop of snow-covered mountains, his gaze confident and optimistic. She knew he was trying to look serious, and older than his sixteen years, but beneath the mustache his lips curved in a half smile, and his brown eyes gleamed with excitement. She knew what he was thinking. Gold!

Nuggets the size of potatoes! Gold lying in a long shining ribbon at the bottom of the creeks, right there for the picking! Why, all it took was a stroll. It was as easy as gathering wildflowers.

"Imagine," she remembered Mother saying the night after Ned left. "We'll be able to pay off the mortgage and buy a new house. We'll live in the lap of luxury. No more taking in washing, not for me. If your father were here, he'd be off with Ned as quick as a whistle. A way out of this economic slump, that's how he'd see it, and off he'd go. Wouldn't he? Well, wouldn't he?"

Only if you pushed him hard enough, Sarah thought. Left to his own devices, her frail and gentle father would no sooner have packed up and headed for the Klondike than he'd've skinned a mule. And Sarah was just the same.

Her thoughts reminded her of a conversation she'd overheard a few nights earlier, when Mother's friends, the Waverleys, came to visit. As always, they'd spent the evening discussing the latest news coming out of the Klondike.

Sarah was almost asleep when she heard Mr. Waverley say, "We're planning to go! It's too late now, what with winter coming, but next spring, you can count Bertha and me amongst the lucky ones!"

Sarah sat up with a start. The Waverleys, off to the Klondike? This was a surprise! Even more surprising was Mother's response. "Oh, Bertha. James. I'd give anything to join you. If it weren't for Sarah being such a handful ... She's at that age, you know. Mind you, we never did see eye-to-eye. She was always her father's girl."

"Bring her along!" Mrs. Waverley said. "Why not, Violet? Could do her the world of good. Might snap her out of that funk she's in."

Mother had laughed. "My Sarah, away from the comforts of home? She wouldn't last a day."

Remembering this, Sarah smiled sadly at the face in the portrait. "She's right, Ned. I wouldn't even last an hour."

As for the "funk" Mrs. Waverley said she was in, that wasn't far wrong either. She had asked her teacher what it meant, to be in a funk, and was told it meant a depressed state of mind. And if a person was called a funk, it meant a coward.

"Not like you, Ned." Sarah sighed and went back to the letter.

> *Sometimes I think I'll never have a real*
> *adventure. But thats all right. You can have one*
> *for both of us.*
> *Love,*
> *Sarah*

She folded the page and added it to the pile of letters she and Mother had already written. No sense in mailing them, not until they knew where Ned was. She could only hope her prayers would reach him, no matter where he might be.

BOAT BUILDING AT LAKE BENNETT, JUNE 17 1898. COPYRIGHT 1898

FALL, 1897

. 7 .

Lake Bennett

Mid-September, 1897

Autumn is at hand. The snowline is getting lower and lower, and fingers of ice are forming in the streams. Everyone's frantic to finish their boats. Tempers are sorely tried ...

"Hand it over, you cheat! Before I blast your scurvy hide clear back to Skagway!"

Ned woke with a start. The shouting he heard was followed by a tremendous thump and holler, as if someone had been knocked into a packing crate. Then he heard a scuffling sound. More thumps, and raucous laughter.

"Not again," he groaned. He turned to face the other side of the tent and pulled a blanket over his ear. But as on the previous five nights, it failed to muffle the noise erupting from the tent next door.

Most of the stampeders who reached Lake Bennett,

either by way of the White Pass or the Chilkoot Pass, were desperate to get their boats built and launched before freeze-up. But a few had decided to spend the winter at the boat-building camp. Among them were three of Montana's friends from Skagway, including the pox-scarred Rooster. They had not only built themselves a log cabin, but had also set up a gambling tent.

"There's gonna be hundreds stuck here," Ned had overheard Rooster remark one day. Ned had been on the lower end of the whipsaw at the time, and with his eyes stinging from the sawdust, he had welcomed the interruption.

"Ain't that right, Montana?" Rooster went on. "Me 'n' the boys, we reckon you should stay out the winter here with us. Hundreds already, more comin' all the time, and nothin' for 'em to do but gamble. Waste o' time goin' to Dawson when there's a fortune to be made right here. So whaddya say?"

"That's some plan," Montana replied, "but I gotta tell ya, Soapy's already come up with a better one. He wants me to set up operations in Dawson."

He must mean that Soapy Smith fellow, Ned thought, the one who helped get back my outfit. And was Montana talking about mining operations? If that was the case, he must be aiming to stake a very large claim. Maybe more than one.

"That's a mean proposition," Rooster declared, "and well worth takin'. But so long as you're here, come 'round to the tent. Play a few hands, bring your cheechako friend."

"Nah, he's cleaned out," Montana said. "But there's plenty more around, wouldn't you say? Anyways, you count me in as a regular. Soon as we quit for the day, I'll be playin' the cards."

Ned shook his head in the darkness of the tent. He wondered how many other stampeders would lose to Montana and his pals. At least he'd learned *his* lesson. Besides, at night he was so exhausted all he wanted to do was sleep. He knew he should write a letter home. But he didn't have the energy to hold a pen, let alone a hand of cards.

Since their arrival at Lake Bennett, Ned had worked frantically — falling trees, whipsawing the green lumber, hammering, caulking and pitching — in a rush to finish his boat and get to the Klondike before freeze-up.

Hurry, hurry, hurry! The air, heavy with the sweet smell of new wood, seemed to call out the words. Hurry, or you won't get through the chain of lakes. Hurry, or you won't float downriver to the goldfields. Hurry, or you'll be stuck at Bennett until spring. Unlike Montana's pals, Ned did not relish the idea of being trapped by winter.

In spite of his earlier intentions, he'd decided to stick with Montana. Two men could build a boat faster than one. Besides, as Montana kept reminding him, where would he be if Montana hadn't bought back his outfit in Skagway? Ned had to pay off his debt. And since he had no money, he had to pay in goods or service or both. All he wished for in return was one night of uninterrupted sleep.

At that moment, another howl burst through the thin walls of the tent. "Soapy's gonna hear about this, you cur!" There was a loud smack and a thud, followed by a moan. "And if you set foot near this tent again, I'll finish you off myself!"

Ned pressed the blanket more tightly to his ear. "Oh, good," he mumbled. "Finish it all off ..." If he was lucky, Montana would change his mind and spend the whole winter at Bennett, taking care of his endless grudges.

At least the boat was finished and almost ready for launching. Ned hated to admit it, but Montana knew a thing or two about boat-building. There were a lot of fellows at the camp who were as handy as a bear when it came to tools. Ned might've fallen into the same category if Montana hadn't helped him along.

One thought nagged at his mind, and during his sleepless hours, he found himself exploring it more and more often. Montana had known a boat had to be built. So why hadn't he brought the necessary tools and supplies? They'd used Ned's whipsaw, Ned's nails and Ned's hammers, and had sealed up the planks with the oakum Ned had hauled over the pass. He couldn't help but wonder what exactly was in Montana's outfit. Come to think of it, it was mostly Ned's beans and bacon they'd been eating lately, too. "Oh, well," he muttered sleepily. "The boat's finished. My debt's paid. Has to be, all things considered." Curled up beside him, Nugget gave a sympathetic yawn.

"Say, Montana!" Rooster's gravelly voice ended a brief moment of quiet. "Whatever happened to that girl you won in a poker game, where was it, down in Seattle? She was a slip of a thing, no more 'n a kid."

Ned let the blanket slip from his ear. The mention of a girl was something different. And had he heard correctly? Had Montana *won* a girl?

Montana gave a loud snort. "That slip of a thing near

bashed my head in."

The men laughed.

"Never thought I'd see the day when a girl'd get the better of Montana Jim!" howled Rooster. "You must be losin' your touch!"

A loud crash followed his words, as if someone had kicked over a box of china. "No one gets the better of me!" Montana bellowed. "Least of all that snively cat! You think she can hit me and get away with it?"

"All due respects, Montana," someone ventured to say, "but it seems like she done just that. You're here on yer own, ain'tcha? No girl in sight. Only that cheechako kid. Say, that was some business in Skagway, waddn't it? Him losin' 'is outfit ..."

More laughter followed. Then they lowered their voices, making comments about cheechakos that Ned couldn't quite hear.

He was about to doze off when he heard another crash, the unmistakeable shatter of glass. He sat up in alarm. Was it a bottle smashed against a crate? Or broken over somebody's head?

"You don't know nothin'!" Montana roared. "That cat took off to the Klondike! Soapy told me, some pal o' his seen her on the wharf in Seattle! Took the first boat outa there! But she ain't gettin' away with it. I'll find her! Why else you think I'm goin' into that godforsaken country? It ain't just on accounta Soapy. That proposition o' his, that's the icing on the cake."

"You gotta hand it to the girl, though," Rooster said. "What is she, fifteen? Sixteen? Imagine, knockin' out

Montana here. Can't say it don't serve 'im right."

The men laughed. Ned braced himself for the thumps that would surely follow this outburst. Was Rooster crazy? Montana would kill him!

Unexpectedly, Montana joined in. But his laughter was short-lived. "We'll see who gets the last laugh," he snarled. "That girl can't hide forever, 'specially not when Soapy's gang's on the lookout."

"Ah, now, Montana, don't be too hard on 'er," someone said.

"Who, me?" Montana chuckled in a nasty way. Then in an abrupt change of tone, he shouted, "Deal us another hand, Roost! We got a game to play, and I'm on a winning streak."

. 8 .

A Stitch in Time

"You're wasting away here, girl."

Catherine looked up at the tailor and raised her eyebrows in a question.

"Not that I mind," Mr. Pendygrasse continued. "You're a fine seamstress, and you've been a great help in the shop. How long's it been now, goin' on two months? But a bright young girl like yourself ... The world's your oyster. Don't let it pass you by."

Catherine gave him a shy smile and went back to her work. What was the expression he'd taught her? *A stitch in time saves nine.* It was true, and not just for sewing. She was going through a waiting time, a settling-in and thinking time. If she struck out now for goodness knows where, she could end up in a worse situation than the one she'd left. Besides, she liked it here. Being hired by Mr. Pendygrasse was the best thing that had ever happened to her. She wouldn't tempt Fate by leaving. She'd landed on a gold mine, and no mistake.

The comparison made her smile. Gold, gold, gold ...
The clamor had not let up. Newspapers were still covered
with gold-driven headlines. Stores springing up along the
waterfront sold nothing but Klondike outfits, and in the
ever-expanding tailor shop, Catherine's work consisted
mainly of sewing flannel overshirts and heavy duck trousers, all destined for the Klondike.

She enjoyed her work, and liked Mr. Pendygrasse. He
remained as gruff and blunt as he'd been the day she walked
into his shop, but he never pried. Nor did Catherine. His
family and friends, his life outside the shop — none of that
was her concern. It was better to keep her distance.

But as the days went by, she thought more about Mr.
Pendygrasse's advice. She began to wonder, Why not? What
did she have to lose? She couldn't hide in the tailor shop
forever. As for the Klondike, what better way to escape
the nightmares of the past than to face a future in the
golden north? No one would think to look for her there.

She began to plan. She saved scraps of material, odds
and ends that might prove useful. A bit of tulle, some canvas,
a square of buckskin to sew into a bag. "A poke for my gold
nuggets," she said as she tucked it away. Then she laughed
and knocked on wood, so that Fate would not be tempted.

When Mr. Pendygrasse heard of her plans, he gave
her a pile of leftover flannel so she could make herself
some overshirts. "It's cold up north," he said, and advised
her to take plenty of warm clothing.

She had months to prepare. It was nearing the end of
October, but she knew from the newspaper accounts,
and from eavesdropping along the waterfront, that no

one could get in or out of the Klondike until the spring break-up. By then she'd have her Klondike outfit and a steamboat ticket. And a new appearance.

She cut her hair short, in the style that was becoming fashionable. She persuaded Mr. Pendygrasse to let her spend even more hours in the shop, and in return for a portion of her wages, she sewed herself some knit under-wear, an extra heavy mackinaw coat and a pair of blanket-lined duck overalls. If she was going to be hiking over a trail, she wouldn't be needing a dress.

Little by little she accumulated the necessary supplies and clothing. A pair of gumboots and woolen mittens. Heavy-soled walking shoes, a wool storm cap. Two gray woolen blankets, a heavy canvas tent. Food provisions could wait until the last minute.

Some mornings she'd go downstairs to the shop and find an unexpected item sitting on her cutting table. A chamois undervest, a cotton nightgown, a wide-brimmed hat. It was obvious that the gifts were from Mr. Pendygrasse, but whenever she tried to thank him he merely grunted, "Best be prepared."

She set her sights on late February as the time to leave Victoria. Up the coast and over the trail — with luck she would reach the lake just as the ice was breaking. After that, it was a mystery. Fate would determine what happened next. She knew better than to plan too far ahead.

She looked forward to her journey, even though it was still months away. But every day brought her closer. Come spring, the girl from the island would be far away. So far, not even the nightmare would find her.

. 9 .

A Race Against the Ice

October, 1897

Left the lakes and entered the river, the last leg of the journey.
Stuck in an ice jam which took nearly all night to get out of.
Continued down the river this morning with great chunks of
ice all around and hardly room to dip our oars in the water ...

The boat was launched. As soon as Ned and Montana
saw that it rode an even keel and didn't leak, they loaded
up and headed across Lake Bennett.

Heavy frost had long since turned the aspen and birch
to gold, and the highbush cranberry glowed red on the
hillsides. Soon the land would be covered with snow, and
ice would be jamming the river. There was not a moment
to lose.

The first strong wind they met ripped away the bril-
liant autumn colours and nearly swamped their boat. Then

came the treacherous Miles Canyon. The fact that they got through the whirlpools and the rapids was due more to luck than to anything else.

Luck stayed with them as they sailed across Lake Laberge and entered the Yukon River. For several days a strong wind and fine current sped them along, and they were able to make good camps for the night.

It was after one such camp, when they were pulling out in the morning, that Ned noticed the ice. Cakes of it were floating downriver, from the upper reaches of the Yukon. "How much farther do we have to go?" he asked nervously. If a boat got caught in the ice, everything, men and all, would be lost.

"Coupla hundred miles," Montana said. "Keep your fingers crossed."

Heavy fog hung above the river, and the snow-covered mountains added to the gloom. At every bend they had to work their way through the ice to the opposite shore in order to reach clear water and float with the rapid current.

The water along the shore was freezing up and staying icebound. But in the deep water, cakes of soft ice were rising to the surface and drifting. As more and more of these slushy cakes appeared, they jostled and smashed and collided until, little by little, they began to freeze into solid blocks.

It wasn't long before snow started to fall. Camps were set up hastily for the night and just as hastily taken down. At Bennett, Ned had gotten hold of a Yukon stove, a heating and cooking contraption that worked much better than his original grate. Once the stove was in place,

Montana threw the opened tent over top, and while Ned pushed the three joints of pipe through the pipe hole in the tent, Montana fastened down the sides. He then supervised as Ned made hot biscuits and heated the beans.

Nugget sat at Ned's feet, eyeing the supper preparations and wagging his tail with anticipation.

"You better pray we make it to Dawson, kid," Montana remarked. "For your mutt's sake, that is."

Ned frowned. "What do you mean?"

"If we're stuck here, is what I mean. If we're frozen in. If we run outa food and can't shoot us a moose or a rabbit. That mutt's gonna make a doggone tasty stew."

Ned turned away quickly and added some bacon to the bean pot. He refused to rise to Montana's bait, no matter how hard the man goaded him. He couldn't afford to have a falling-out now. He needed an extra pair of hands to get him the rest of the way, especially with the ice closing in.

The next day the river was so full of ice they had no choice but to drift with the floes, using their oars to push the ice away from the boat so it wouldn't get crushed. For three days they drifted, wielding their oars until they were worn down to pointed sticks. On the fourth day, they reached the confluence of the Klondike and Yukon rivers. Here, too, the Yukon was full of ice — upended blocks and crags that smashed and jammed and froze in a solid, white-turquoise mass.

"Stay in the center!" Montana yelled. "We're almost there, but if we get off to the side we're stuck!"

Ned was well aware of the danger. The ice had already

seized dozens of boats, some standing on end, prows down, others on their sides.

In the distance he could see the patch of shale some old-timers had told him about. It had been torn out of the wooded hillside by an ancient slide, and looked like a huge moosehide stretched out to dry. He could also see a settlement beneath the hill, a jumble of log structures and tents that sprawled along the riverbank.

And boats! He thought they'd had a good head start from Bennett, but many had beaten them to it. Scows were lined up three and four deep, tied one behind the other in a wobbly clutter that stretched from the mouth of the Klondike to Moosehide Hill. They were all left to the ice now, most abandoned by men who'd gone tearing off to the goldfields. A few were rigged with tarpaulins and looked as though they'd be someone's living quarters for the winter. There was no getting out of the Klondike now.

"Push, Buckingham!" Montana cried. "Stop gazing at the scenery and push!"

Ned pushed and strained against the massive blocks until he thought his oar might snap. They were almost there ...

Suddenly a huge block reared up at the prow. The boat groaned and creaked, then leaned on its side, pushed over by the tremendous build-up of ice. They were held fast.

"This is it, kid," Montana said. "The ice has got us beat."

Ned let out a large sigh. With fingers shaking from cold and excitement, he took out his diary and wrote the long-awaited entry. *October 27, 1897 — I'm one of the lucky ones. I've arrived in Dawson City!*

The first step was unloading his outfit. Then off to the goldfields! The thought kept him going as he staggered across the jagged piles of ice, hauling one load after another. But when his goods were finally stacked on the riverbank, Montana confounded him by saying, "Payback time, kid! You can come work for me in the Blue Spruce Saloon and I'll take it off your wages. Or you can let me have what's left of your outfit."

"What?" Ned gaped. "I don't owe you anything! I worked on the boat, I supplied the nails and the pitch and all the tools, you've eaten most of my grub — what's this about payback time? And a saloon? You said you were staking a claim!"

"Don't recall I did, Buckingham. Nope, that musta been an assumption on your part. Thing is, I come up here to run the saloon. That 'n' the gambling. Heck, why would I bother mining for gold when I can mine the miners?"

He laughed heartily, then slapped a beefy arm across Ned's shoulders. "Don't look so discouraged, Bucko. Pay me back and we're square."

"I just — I can't —"

"Ooh ... You just, you can't!" he mocked. "Kid, you're breakin' my heart. But I'm a reasonable man. What say you keep your outfit, and give me whatever money you got."

Ned fished deep into his pocket for his one remaining dollar, then threw the crumpled bill at Montana. "Take it. And I hope I never see you again."

He was about to turn away when a man approached and greeted Montana warmly. "Thank goodness you made it before freeze-up," he said. "We was thinkin' we might have to face the winter without any whiskey. You get the whole shipment through?"

Montana glanced over at Ned and winked. "Thanks to Sir Buckingham, here. These cheechakos, they're better 'n a horse any day."

"Well, load 'er up and let's get to the bar. Hey, boys!" he yelled to a group of men across the street. "Bring the wagon over here!"

Ned stared at Montana's outfit, speechless. All those packs and crates — they couldn't be filled with whiskey. He would've heard the bottles clinking. They would've been smashed to bits the way they were handled on the trail.

Montana must have read his thoughts because he clapped Ned on the shoulder and said, "You want a drop o' whiskey for the road?"

Ned continued to gape as Montana opened a crate and stepped aside. "Have a closer look, partner. Whaddya think?"

Ned was stunned. The crate was full of whiskey, all right. What was even worse, every bottle was packed in hay. "Your — your horse," he stammered. "That poor horse, you let him starve. And the whole time, you had all this, this — How *could* you? And what about the customs? When we had to stop between the lakes —"

"You wonder how I got by the Customs House? Heck, Soapy ain't the only one who's slipp'ry. And there was quite the blizzard at the time, if you recall. Hey, don't look so glum! I let you keep the dog."

Ned turned away in disgust. "Come on, Nugget," he said. Just then, Montana flung out his foot and gave the dog a parting kick in the side. Nugget instantly spun around and faced Montana, his teeth bared and a threatening growl building in his throat.

"No, boy!" Ned called out. "He's not worth the trouble." He headed off down the street with Nugget at his heels.

Ned was relieved to be free of Montana, but now that he'd reached the end of his journey, he wasn't sure what to do next. He'd intended to head for the goldfields, but where exactly were they? He hadn't seen a sign saying, This way to the gold. And if the competition on the trail was any indication, there weren't going to be a lot of fellows eager to point the way.

He was alone, a cheechako. He probably looked as naive and vulnerable as he felt. He'd already been taken in by Montana and his cronies, but he was determined it wouldn't happen again. Maybe his best bet was to have a look around town, get his bearings, then think of a plan.

Dawson City was smaller than he'd expected, although there had obviously been a lot of building going on over the summer. Front Street, the main street that ran along the riverbank, was lined with rough-lumber shacks, company stores and low structures covered with corrugated iron. There were tent stores and tent hotels, as well as saloons, dance halls and restaurants. Only one of the restaurants, the Fireweed Cafe, was open. The rest were closed because their provisions were gone. The warehouses, too, were nearly empty, except for staples like flour, rice, bacon and beans.

"Good news, eh, Nugget? If we run out of beans, we can buy some more beans." The thought made him groan.

The call of the wild might be a timber wolf's howl to some folks, but to him it was the rumbling belch from a perpetually sour stomach.

The snow-covered hillside behind the town had a scattering of white canvas tents, a forest of stumps and several small, newly built log cabins. A few high trees remained at the northern edge. Behind them Ned could see more clearly the moosehide patch of shale.

There were no sidewalks in town, only a network of trails. He followed one as far as the North West Mounted Police post, where a number of log houses had been arranged around three sides of a square. A quick look showed they were used for quarters and storerooms, a post office, courtroom and other government offices. The fourth side faced the Yukon.

Ned swallowed his disappointment. After months of hard travel and anticipation, this was it? A river, some hills and a few log cabins? It was scarcely a town, much less a city. As for the prospectors, the ones he'd passed on the so-called street looked as grim and disheartened as he felt. Were these the millionaires he'd read about with such excitement? Surely not.

One thing was certain. The letter he thought he'd be writing to Mother and Sarah, telling them about the glorious discovery he'd made on arrival, would have to wait. He couldn't tell them the truth. They might think what a part of him was already thinking – he'd made a terrible mistake.

Typical, Father would have said. Another example of your high-flying ideas coming to naught. When are you going to grow up ...

Ned gave a loud sigh. He no longer had to answer to his father. But he did have to answer to himself. And thanks to the weather, the part of him that longed to turn back and go home was forced to stay and persevere.

A plan began to form in his mind. Before making his way to the goldfields, he'd find a spot on the hillside and set up his tent. Then he'd spend some time talking to people, especially to the experienced prospectors. Things couldn't be as bad as they appeared. He was tired, that's all. Tired and depressed and frustrated after his daily dealings with Montana. He'd talk to the real prospectors. And listen to what they had to say.

. 10 .

Grim News

Early November, 1897

The news is grim. All the creeks are staked. The whole country is staked, for 200 miles around Dawson ...

"You can't be serious!" Ned exclaimed. "You don't mean — *All* the creeks are staked? But I thought —"

"I know what you thought." Frosty Jack Thurston, a white-haired prospector Ned had met at the Fireweed Cafe, nodded sympathetically and slurped his coffee. "You thought you beat the rush. You thought there'd be gold lying around as thick as wheat on a prairie field. 'Course, that's not to say a person *can't* get lucky. That's placer mining for you. All you need is a pick and a shovel, a pan and some water. A cheechako like you might strike it rich, whereas a sourdough like myself might have trouble finding enough dust to buy his daily food. Nature has no favorites.

But like I was saying, all the good ground is gone."

Ned idly stirred his coffee, thinking of the endless line of gold seekers struggling over the White Pass Trail. The trail would likely be closed for the winter, but the line would resume in the spring. The same would be true on the Chilkoot Trail. All the stampeders would converge at Lake Bennett, build their boats and wait for the ice to thaw. Then they'd head for Dawson, thousands upon thousands. He groaned. "I've come all this way for nothing. Now I'm trapped."

"You could come work for wages on my claim," Frosty Jack said. "It's a rich one, staked on Bonanza Creek last summer, right after the big discovery. I'm heading back out tomorrow and I could sure use an extra hand over the winter. Later on, if you've a mind, you could venture farther off into the hills and try your luck. Question is, have you got lots of food? They're expecting a shortage, 'cause the supply boats haven't made it. They won't, neither, now that the river's froze."

When Ned assured him he had enough food for the winter, Frosty Jack went on with his proposal. "I got a pack train going out to the creeks tomorrow. Gotta buy some lumber first, and a few supplies for the missus. You're welcome to load up your outfit and come along if you want a winter job. There's an empty cabin you can move into, save you the trouble of building your own. And I see you got a dog for company. A fella can go mad out there with no one to talk to. Even if it's only a dog." He patted Nugget on the head.

"Now, about your wages. There's other fellas working

on my claim, and I'll pay you the same as I pay them, an ounce of gold a day. That's sixteen dollars for a ten-hour day, and it's paid in gold dust, like everything else around here."

What choice do I have? Ned wondered. He could go further afield, but with winter fast approaching, and him being on his own ... He held out his hand. "I'm obliged, Mr. Thurston."

"Call me Frosty Jack. We don't take to formalities, not around here." He gave Ned's hand a firm shake.

They set out on horseback the next morning, leading a train of six mules loaded with lumber and supplies. It wasn't long before Ned discovered that Frosty Jack was a wealth of information — and advice.

"First thing you gotta do, son, is shave off your whiskers and mustache. You notice how clean-shaven I am? A smooth face is a positive comfort come winter. When you get moisture from your breath freezing in a mustache and beard, it's as painful a trial in winter as the mosquito in summer. And when you're asleep, you risk the chance of suffocating if it freezes 'round your mouth and nose."

"I thought a beard would keep your face warmer," Ned said. "That's why I've been growing one."

Frosty Jack chuckled. "You'll learn. You're a cheechako now, but you'll be a sourdough soon. It's going on ten years since I been a newcomer like yourself. Ten years since I first saw the freeze-up in autumn and the break-up in spring. Yessir, it's been a long time ..."

Ned listened with interest as Frosty Jack talked about his early days in the Klondike, how he and his wife had prospected all over the hills. And how, after the discovery of 1896, he'd been one of the first to stake not only on Bonanza, but also on lower Eldorado, where another big discovery had been made.

"That's how it is," he explained. "Soon as a discovery is made, you tell everyone. 'Cause the person that makes the discovery can't stake anywhere else on the same creek. They just get the discovery claim. But they know that other prospectors on other creeks might strike gold and tell them. So that way they get a chance somewhere else. That's how come I got two good claims. Just in time, too, 'cause now the Dominion's got a law saying a man can only stake on one creek in the whole district. But they're all gone, the good ones. And that's why all them cheechakos coming up here are out o' luck."

They rode in silence for a while, across the frozen Klondike and up Bonanza Creek. "Those evergreens —" Ned pointed to a stand of dark trees shaped like Christmas trees. "We used them for the boat but I've forgotten their name."

"Spruce," said Frosty Jack. "And I'll let you in on a little secret. Consider yourself lucky, son, 'cause I don't tell every cheechako, but spruce needle tea, that's the ticket. Throw out your coffee or give it to me, don't much matter. But you drink spruce needle tea. And lots of it."

"Why?" It sounded dreadful.

"To keep off the scurvy. That'll kill you if you're not careful. Unless you brought a load of fresh fruit and vegetables. No? How about canned vegetables and dried fruit?"

"I did, but it's almost all gone." Pilfered away by that rat Montana.

"How about lime tablets? Or citric acid?"

Ned shook his head guiltily, remembering how he'd scoffed when his mother had suggested taking citric acid along with cod-liver oil.

"Well, then. You stick to spruce needle tea. My other bit of advice is sourdough bread."

"I've never heard of sour dough."

"You're hearing it now, so pay attention. You ate baking-powder bread coming up here, I'll wager. Well, forget it. It's easier to make, but for a good diet, sourdough bread's the ticket. On account of the yeast, you see."

Ned couldn't help but smile. He'd been expecting an earful of advice about gold mining, not nutrition.

Frosty Jack laughed. "Oh, I can see you think I'm a demented old prospector, nothing to do but count my gold nuggets, chow down on the sourdough bread, swill a bitter brew of spruce needles. I admit it sounds kinda funny. But I tell anyone who works on my mine the same thing. Selfish reasons, of course. I don't have an ounce of humanitarian spirit if you want the truth, 'specially not toward cheechakos coming up here and thinking they know it all. Nope, I tell 'em so they don't get sick and quit on me. So there you have it." He turned to Ned and grinned. "Now then, anything else you want to know?"

Ned was surprised by the question that came into his mind. Here he was, finally on his way to the goldfields, to the world-famous Bonanza Creek, and what did he ask? How a person made that sourdough bread.

He'd pass on the instructions to Mother and Sarah as soon as he got around to writing home. It was bound to make them laugh, the picture of Ned up to his elbows in sour dough. He hoped it would make up for the picture they wouldn't see — the one of Ned strolling through the goldfields, picking up nuggets by the handful.

. 11 .

Twice a Fool

Mid-November, 1897

Here I am at Bonanza Creek. My first day underground ...

"Don't mind the fumes." Frosty Jack gasped and coughed as he spoke. "It's smoky work, no getting around it."

Ned followed the older man down the sturdy green-birch ladder, choking on the fumes that filled the underground shaft. It was a shock to learn that working on a gold mine meant digging underground. He *should* have known. After all, he'd brought the required pick and shovel. What was he planning to do, use them to decorate his cabin? He cursed himself for being so naive.

"It's all a matter of finding the paystreak," Frosty Jack said. "And to do that, you gotta get below and dig. On a good claim like this, there's usually a certain amount of gold lying on the surface, easy to get by panning. So some of them rumors you heard was true. But picking out the gold's like skimming grease from a stew pot. Most of the riches stays underground."

"How far down do we dig?" It seemed like they'd been descending forever.

"Straight down to the bedrock, some fifteen, eighteen feet. Sometimes you go down as much as thirty feet."

"But the ground's frozen solid! It's —" Ned searched for the term he'd recently heard. "Permafrost!"

"I know that!" Frosty Jack laughed. "So you have to soften it up. Thaw it out. Build a fire. And keep that fire going night and day. When the ground's soft enough, you force your way through with a pick. That's how we work a claim in the winter. Burn out the hole, put the pay dirt aside, and wash it come spring when the creek starts to flow.

"Chilblains, the fella down below, he does the digging once the fire's softened things up. Then he fills a box. Skipper, the fella you met up top at the windlass, he hoists up the box o' diggings and dumps it. That's what all them piles are, on the surface. We call 'em the dumps.

"Mind your head, now. We're squeezing down this tunnel." A few feet into the tunnel Frosty Jack stopped and lit a candle. "This here's the paystreak, what used to be the old creek bed. Can you see the pay?"

Ned's eyes gleamed. Even through the smoke he could see the glittering flakes of gold.

Frosty Jack took out his pocket knife and dug out a few nuggets, the largest the size of a bean. "I expect this piece of ground'll fetch me a hundred thousand dollars," he remarked casually. Then he clapped a hand on Ned's shoulder and wished him well.

Ned worked for several hours. It was during the lunch break, while chatting with Skipper and Chilblains, that he had another shock.

"The closest town here is Grand Forks," Chilblains was saying, "so you don't need to go all the way to Dawson. They got everything in Grand Forks. Restaurants, saloons, hotels, even a post office."

"Do they have a telegraph office?" Ned wondered. "They had one in Skagway. It was expensive to send a telegram but I —"

"You sent one anyway?" The men slapped their knees and hooted with laughter.

Ned looked from one to the other, puzzled.

"Someone pulled your leg but good!" Skipper exclaimed. "There ain't no telegraph wires in Alaska, let alone a genuine office!"

Ned felt like kicking himself. From the moment Montana laid eyes on him, that first day on the steamboat, he'd had Ned pegged as an easy mark. Cheechako? Try chump. Try monumental idiot. As for Mother and Sarah, what must they be thinking? Here it was November, and the only message he'd sent was that phony telegram, way back in August. He couldn't put it off any longer.

That night, as soon as he finished supper, he put pen to paper and wrote his first letter home.

Bonanza Creek, near Grand Forks
November 15, 1897

Dear Mother and Sarah,
 How are you? I hope you are both well. I
apologize for not writing sooner.
 At long last I have reached the Klondike.
I'm in the goldfields, working on a claim, but
I'm sorry to say it's not mine.
 I thought it would be easy, just find a
nearby creek and pick up the nuggets. But
everything's all staked. I'm working for wages,
for a Jack Thurston who has a rich claim on
Bonanza Creek. Rich as it is, we still don't
pick up the nuggets. We dig down twenty feet
through frozen muck and bedrock until we hit
the gravel. Then we dig out the gravel. That's
where the gold is, if you're lucky enough to find
it. It turns out I am not one of the lucky ones.
 Whoever comes to the Klondike in
ignorance, like I did, is a fool. And to come
alone, without friend or family, is twice a fool.
I would not advise any person to come. If half
the people get here that are likely on the trail, I
have no idea what they will do or where they
will go. There's no room for them in Dawson.
I suppose there's lots of gold left somewhere in
the hills. The only trouble is to find it.
Everything is chance.
 I wish I had a happy tale to tell. The only

bit of gold I found is a mutt I rescued in Skagway. I call him Nugget. And what a faithful friend he's turned out to be.

If you want to picture where I am, imagine a log cabin with a wooden floor and a door so low I have to stoop to get inside. The cracks between the logs are chinked with mud and moss, and there's a sod roof. Frosty Jack (that's what we call Mr. Thurston), he tells me that in the spring I'll be able to pick wild raspberries right off my roof. But right now it's covered with snow.

There's not much furniture since lumber is too expensive to buy. The miner who built the cabin broke apart his scow to make a wall bunk, some shelves and a table. I use my packing crates for chairs and cupboards. It's a luxury cabin compared to some, on account of the soda-bottle windows.

There's a large Yukon range in the corner, with a pipe that goes up through the roof. I strung up two lines in the cabin. One's over the stove to hang my socks so they'll dry, and the other's to keep the frozen slab of bacon away from the mice. So that's my home sweet home.

What I mostly eat is Alaska strawberries. Before you get too envious, that's what we call beans that aren't cooked right through. On account of the pink color.

On one of the shelves I've got a jar of sourdough starter that Mr. Thurston's wife gave me. It's made from potato water and flour and salt and sugar. To make the sourdough bread you add more flour, let it rise, then you bake it. But you always keep back a half cup of the starter so you can make more bread another time. Or pancakes or doughnuts. The starter's supposed to last forever. It'll be a treat for you both!

I forgot to mention there's a huge tin basin leaning up against the wall. One of these days I'm going to heat up enough water to have a good long soak. You don't want to know the last time I had a proper bath.

It's hard to describe this country. There are mountains, rivers, creeks, snow and ice. I've been walking on snow and ice ever since I came in. A month from now it will be more of the same, only colder. I have seen the Aurora borealis, the northern lights, and a more eerie spectacle you cannot imagine.

I promise I will write a longer letter when I'm not so bushed. A letter from you both would be most welcome. Now that you know where to send it I will be waiting anxiously.

Your loving son and brother,
Ned

*(The miners around here call me Long
Shanks because I'm so tall. I swear I grew
another two inches on the trail.)*

It wasn't until the end of November that Ned finally
got around to taking the letter to the post office in Grand
Forks. By that time he had added a much lengthier description of his journey, as well as his feelings about the
place. The clerk took the letter, postmarked the envelope
November twenty-fifth and jokingly assured him it would
reach Victoria by Easter, if not by Christmas.

WINTER, 1897–98

. 12 .

It Won't Be A Merry Christmas

Victoria, December 21, 1897

Dear Ned,
 *Today is my 13th birthday. I am very sad
that your not here. Mother is sad too. We keep
wondering why you haven't written and even if
your still alive. So please write and tell us
where you are. Then we'll send such a big stack
of letters that the post man will need a whole
team of dogs to deliver them to your door.*
 *In Victoria everybody's still got gold rush
fever. Like the Waverleys. There leaving at the end
of February and never talk about anything else.
Mother listens and goes dreamy-eyed. And she
scolds ME for daydreaming. Sometimes she even
gets tears in her eyes because she's thinking of
you. (Me too.)*

*The streets here are clogged with people
planning to go north because if they buy there
outfits here they don't have to pay duty or
something like that. So you were smart to go
from here. (But where else would you go from,
ha ha.) The store where you were working
before you quit has a big sign saying Klondike
Outfitters. Like all the other stores. There all
filled with mocasins and boots and sleighs and
cures for frostbite. I hope you havent got
frostbite.*

*There's no chance of getting frostbite here.
Some mornings have been a bit frosty but
mostly its rain, rain, rain. I think of you in the
snow. It must be nice. And fun. Do you have
time to go sledding? Do you go on sleigh rides?*

*I look at your portrait and imagine you in
your cozy cabin counting your nuggets. Mother
says that's why you have'nt written, your to
busy. She also heard the post is very slow.*

*It's almost Christmas but it won't be a
merry one without Father and now without
you. Mother is helping with the church supper
and I'm singing in the choir at school and at
church. And helping with decorations. Mother
says we can put up a little tree at home, even
though she says her heart isn't in it. But I think
a cheery tree with the candles lit will help our
spirits. Will you have a Christmas tree in your
cabin? Do they have lots of trees up there?*

What will you have for Christmas dinner? Mother says she hopes you saved the shortbread but you probably gobbled it up ages ago. If I know you.

I'll tell you a secret. I'm going to wrap up your present and you can open it as soon as you come home. I pray that it will be soon. Sometimes I think you have'nt written because your on your way this very minute and just want to surprize us! That would make this the best Christmas ever.

Love,
Sarah

. 13 .

The Dead of Winter

January, 1898

A brand new year. I have no idea what I will do in the dark days ahead. Ever since Christmas my spirits have been that low.

I don't have half the strength I had a month ago, even a week ago. I'm near breathless with exhaustion and every day that comes is back-breaking work. You build the fire and keep it burning ten hours at a time. If you're way down deep and the fire starts to blaze, you climb up quick or suffocate. Even if you're quick enough, you're gasping for air at the top.

When the fire burns down you go back into the tunnel to shovel the ashes. Then pick, pick, pick at the earth, loosen it up, dig out the clumps, fill the buckets, hoist them up to the dump.

I wasn't working two weeks when Frosty Jack decided to sink a new hole. It took a month to dig down 15 feet, picking through the muck, as hard as ice and so tough it wore down a pick in minutes. Then I got to the paystreak and drifted sideways for another few weeks. Same routine. Build the fire, soften the ground, and dig.

Frosty Jack has all the luck. Some miners I heard about sunk five holes and never hit the paystreak. Some miners spent a whole year digging without a speck of color to show for it. And on another claim, ten feet away, a man could be picking out nuggets bigger than the calluses on his hands.

The dumps keep getting higher. They look like ancient burial mounds, or heaps of concrete. All covered with snow. There's plenty of gold nuggets hidden inside. But no danger of anyone stealing the gold. Ten minutes after the gravel is dumped, it's frozen so hard it's safer than in a bank. And you can hardly see anything anyway ...

Winter hung over the valley.

The cold was a constant invader, attacking with every breath. Thirty below, forty below, fifty below ... For several days the intense cold brought all work to a halt. No one dared stir out of their cabins.

The snow was deep, and so light and dry it flew up when you walked, like feathers. It fell in a fine, crystalline dust, swirling the landscape with cold white smoke. It never melted. Each new snowfall piled another layer on top of the last, so as the weeks progressed, the cushion underfoot became softer and deeper. And the snow was never silent. The sounds varied underfoot, from high-pitched squeaks to the low hollow thrum of a drumbeat.

Darkness stole over the mountains, along the creeks and into the cabins. By December the sun had virtually disappeared.

Ned's world was a landscape of darkness, broken only by a purple twilight, the red glow of fires, the yellow flames of candles. A darkness brightened by moonlight and the glaze of snow.

It was a world of shadowy figures that drifted through the valley from cabin to cabin, from claim to claim, their muffled voices rising and falling like the wails of ghosts, eerie and forlorn.

And when the day's digging was done, when the men vanished into the gauzy veils of snow, the ghost voices stole inside Ned's cabin. They hounded him as he huddled by his stove, and took shape in the steam rising from his damp clothes. And the voices wailed, "Why have you come? Why are you here? Go home, go home, go home ..."

"I can't!" Ned shouted. He pounded the air with his fists to beat away the ghosts, but they would not let him be. They crept into his sleep and into his dreams. "You do not belong here," they wailed. "Go home, go home ..." And Ned would wake to find tears frozen on his cheeks.

One night, as he was dragging himself home, he heard a soft hissing, like the rustle of silk. It was a sound he associated with the northern lights. From the moment he'd first seen them, he'd greeted the sound with wonder and delight. This time he clapped his hands to his ears and hollered up at the sky, "Go away! Stop tormenting me!"

Instead of retreating, the lights drew closer. Green-white ghost lights, they taunted Ned with faint, crackling voices. "Too late, too late... You'll never go home. You're trapped in the ice and the snow and the dark. You're trapped in the cold. And there is no gold, no gold for you ..."

"Stop!" Ned screamed. "Go away!"

They would not stop. They swirled and shimmered in long sweeping rolls, so close to the earth, Ned stopped breathing for fear they would reach out and touch him. Then, at the last moment, they rolled up to the stars and danced another sweeping rhythm across the sky. "Next time we'll take you," they laughed. "There's only one way home ..."

"Leave me alone!" Desperate to escape, Ned staggered into his cabin, slammed the door and collapsed on his bunk. His legs throbbed with pain. His heart raced. Sweat poured down his forehead.

There was no escape. The walls of his cabin whirled in and out and the ghost voices murmured, "Come away, come away ..."

One voice was familiar. "Father?" Ned whispered. "Is that you? I'm sorry. I'm sorry I let you down." His voice broke with sobs.

Nugget placed his head on Ned's lap and whimpered softly.

"I'll take you home, boy." Ned leaned forward and buried his face in the dog's fur. Then he stretched out on his bunk and covered himself with a blanket. If he could fall asleep, everything would be fine. He'd wake up and be home.

He was about to doze off when he heard the distant jingling of harness bells. "Someone's coming," he muttered. "They'll need a fire. And food. And warm clothes."

He stumbled from the bunk and only then realized how cold the cabin was. Why hadn't he lit a fire? As for warm clothes, his own clothes had become soaked with sweat and had since frozen stiff. He'd have to do something about that, and quickly. But first, the fire.

Light, matches ... He rummaged through a packing crate until he found a candle. "Come on, come on ..." His fingers were so numb he couldn't grip the matches, let alone strike one. Putting his mittens back on didn't help. They, too, were frozen. He worked his hands inside his shirt, held them under his armpits and, ignoring the pain in his legs and feet, stamped around the cabin in an effort to get the circulation going. When he was finally able to move his fingers, he lit the candle, then managed to open his knife blade. He clamped his fingers around the handle and prepared some shavings for kindling. Then he stuffed the shavings under some wood and lit them with the candle flame.

"What'll we have, Nugget? Hey, boy? What is it that Frosty Jack's always raving about? Some kind of tea. Juice beetle tea, that's it. So we need water ..." He broke an icicle from an inside corner of the cabin and put it in the kettle to melt. Then he set a pot of beans and bacon on the stove and, after changing out of his frozen clothes, hunkered down on a crate in front of the stove.

Nugget gazed up at him and whined.

"Hush, boy. I've got to listen. Do you hear the bells?

Have the guests arrived?" He strained to hear the harness bells, but they were gone. The valley was heavy with silence.

The stove was heating up, but it was no match for the cold. Ned's front was red-hot, but his back was as cold as ice, in spite of his two wool shirts and sheepskin coat. "How many more days of this?" he said. "Hey, Nugget? Days and weeks and months ..." First, tonight. If he could get through this one night ...

As soon as the beans were heated through, he and Nugget would gulp them down. They would have to eat fast, otherwise the food would freeze. Then he'd crawl into his sleeping bag, pull the three heavy blankets on top and sleep. One more night. Then another. Weeks and months of nights. And days as dark as night. If he fell asleep and never woke up it would be a blessing.

"There's an easier way."

Ned looked around in alarm. Was it the murmur of the wind he heard? Or something else? "Who's there?" he cried. "Show yourself!"

Shadows flared up and swirled in the wavering candlelight.

"Is that you?" A thin, ghost-like shape loomed against the far wall. Ned drew back in fear, but when he blinked, he saw it was his clothes, hanging from a spike in the wall.

"An easier way ..." The voice gave a haunting laugh.

Another shape flapped in the draft blowing in through the cracks.

"I see you now!" But a sputtering from the candle revealed Ned's long johns, steaming above the stove.

Hunched-over shadows huddled on the floor beside

the door. Ned rubbed his eyes and saw they were no more than half-empty sacks of flour and rice.

The voice laughed again. "Make it easy ..."

"Who are you?" Ned cried. "Why can't you leave me alone?"

"See the rope against the wall? Throw it over the beam. Make the loop. Move some crates. Make it easy ... You will never be cold or tired or hungry again."

"Get out!" Ned shouted. "Leave me alone!"

"You will never be lonely. You will be home ..."

Suddenly it was too much. Ned covered his face with his hands and sobbed with despair.

Nugget whined and scratched at the door. He pawed Ned's shoulder and licked his hands in an effort to rouse him. When there was no response he barked frantically, then tugged at the corner of Ned's coat.

All Ned could see was the shadow. All he could hear was the voice. "Make it easy, lad. End it this way, like I did."

Ned raised his head and looked around the dismal cabin. "Now I know!" he cried. "You're the old prospector. You built this wretched place."

"You think it's wretched now?" the voice replied. "Wait a month. And another month. And another after that. Spring is a lifetime away. Summer's a dream ..."

A gust of wind shrieked through a crack and blew out the candle. The room plunged into a deeper darkness.

Ned focused his gaze on the red glow of the stove. His aching body now burned with a feverish heat, yet he couldn't stop shaking.

And here was Mother. Had she come on the sleigh

with the jingling bells? Father was with her, too. And Sarah. They were turning up their noses, saying what a miserable place it was, filthy, and riddled with mouse droppings. How it reeked! And not just the cabin. Ned smelled to high heaven. As for his appearance! His hair was as long and shaggy as the dog's, he was plagued with lice, he couldn't stop scratching, he should be ashamed. And where was the gold?

"I didn't find it!" Ned sobbed. "I made a mistake, I never should have come!"

"Oh, Ned." Father's face was a mask of sorrow and disappointment. "Didn't I always tell you, look before you leap?"

"Oh, God, I'm sorry."

"Give up, son. Quit now. You always were one to quit when things got too rough. The easy way, Ned. You always took the easy way. Come home with us now."

They all spoke at once, their voices rising and falling until he couldn't tell where one stopped and the others began. One voice finally broke clear. The prospector's, telling him what he had to do.

It was easy. The rope. The loop. The beam. The crates.

With fumbling fingers, Ned followed the instructions. He was almost there ...

No, there was one last thing to do. He opened the cabin door so the dog could get out. A part of his mind wondered how the dog had come to be there in the first place. Had Sarah brought it? He wished it would stop barking.

Shakily, he stumbled on to the crates, stood up and

adjusted the rope. He closed his eyes and murmured what he thought was a prayer. In the distance he heard the ringing of bells. Then, like before, they faded away, echoing across the vast expanse of snow.

. 14 .

Unexpected News

It was a cold January day when Sarah came home from school and heard the news that would set her world spinning.

Her mother greeted her at the door with such a glow on her face, Sarah immediately cried, "It's Ned, isn't it? We've finally got a letter! He's on his way home!"

"Better than that, dear," Mother said. She reached out her arms and embraced Sarah so tightly Sarah thought her ribs might crack.

"What? What is it, then?"

"We're going to the Klondike, Sarah! You and me! And the Waverleys! We'll all travel together. I've bought the steamboat tickets and made a deposit on the outfits. We leave the end of February. It's all arranged."

"Mother! You — we can't!" Sarah stepped back, her face a mixture of bewilderment and concern. She had never seen her mother so excited, but what on earth was she thinking? She was mad! The fact they hadn't heard from Ned in five months had made her completely crazy. "You're not — No! We just can't!"

"Oh yes, we can! And don't give me the gloomy look. Be happy! You know how you love to read adventure stories. Now here's your chance to live one!"

"No!" Sarah retorted. "You can't be serious! I — I won't last a day in the Klondike. I'm too dull. And stodgy. You said so yourself."

"Whenever did I say that? I certainly didn't mean it."

"Well, you did. And what about school?"

"Never mind about school." Mother waved her hand in a dismissive gesture. "You'll catch up when you get home, a smart girl like yourself. Now, come along, don't just stand there gaping. Get your coat off, have some tea, and I'll tell you the plans."

She bustled about the kitchen, putting the water on to boil, then setting out milk and sugar and biscuits. "You know," she said as Sarah sat down, "it's not as though it's unheard of. Every day there's ladies and children bound for the North. I read it in the papers. See this?" She passed Sarah a clipping that listed all the items a woman traveler should take to the Klondike. "We'll have plenty of female companions. And besides, it will give us a chance to have a special experience together. We haven't always got along, I know. Especially since your dear father ... but honestly, Sarah, it'll do us both the world of good."

Sarah looked at her mother and saw not only excitement but determination. She knew in her heart there'd be no going back. Mother was a doer. She wouldn't change her mind, not unless Ned came home.

"Well ..." She sighed. "I suppose I could manage. If I have to."

"That's the spirit!" Mother clapped her hands in delight. "And we'll find that boy of ours, won't we? That Ned! Something's not right. I feel it in my bones."

The next few weeks passed in a flurry. There was so much packing to do and so many things to think about. And then, three nights before their departure, something happened that made Sarah's world spin even faster.

They were at a potluck supper, given by the church to wish them a safe and prosperous journey. It was an evening of good cheer and laughter, and in spite of herself, Sarah was beginning to feel excited. But as they were leaving, the unthinkable happened. Mother slipped on the icy steps of the church hall, fell to the ground and broke her hip.

There was no question of her going anywhere, let alone to the Klondike. In a frenzy of decision-making, she sold her ticket and outfit for double what she'd spent, gave the money to Sarah, and arranged for the Waverleys to take Sarah with them.

"I can't!" Sarah cried. "I'm only thirteen! And what about you? Who'll look after you?"

"Don't worry, I'm in good hands. The ladies from the church are taking care of me." She reached up from her bed and wiped away Sarah's tears. "Please, Sarah. Don't make it more difficult. I want you to go. The Waverleys are like family. It's not as if I'm sending you off on your own. And you'll find Ned and bring him home. At least find out why the rascal hasn't written. And give him a piece of my mind."

Sarah tried to hold back a fresh outburst of tears, but couldn't. "I don't *want* to go! I *never* wanted to go!"

"Sarah," Mother said firmly. "I said it to Ned and I'll say it to you. It's the chance of a lifetime. And you know it, even though you won't admit it. This last month, as we were getting ready, I saw a spark of life in your eyes I haven't seen since before your father died. You're too young to lose that spark. You go north, and get it back."

She paused to wipe her own eyes with a handkerchief, then laughed. "Funny, isn't it? You're off to the frozen north, and what keeps me from going? A patch of ice, here in temperate Victoria."

. 15 .

An Open Door

The walls were alive, swarming with hands and arms and legs and feet, faces and voices, thumps and groans and sighs.

In the midst of the confusion, Ned heard someone ranting about juicy beetles and ghosts and going home.

As the voice rambled on, he felt himself being lifted and carried across a sunlit field. The voice cried out, "Father! I did it so you'd be proud! I did it for cold in the glondike ..."

He was on his back, stretched out on the grass at the edge of the field. Hands and arms disappeared, faces swam in and out of focus, eyes blinked and peered. "Father? Is that you? Are we home?"

He heard a man speaking, but it wasn't Father. "Same thing happened to mosquitoes. He's delirious."

Delirious? Who was Delirious? Funny name for a man. And he mentioned mosquitoes. Was it summer? Was that why he was so hot? The mosquitoes hadn't bitten him, except on the neck and face, and even inside his mouth. His lips felt swollen, his gums were tender, and his throat was a thousand times too big. Was that from mosquitoes? It was too hard to think ...

Some time later, he woke up and found he was in a cabin. It was filled with light and activity. Men were chopping wood, filling kettles, lighting candles, preparing grub. Their voices were different than the ones he'd heard before, the voices of those who had taken him home. But that couldn't be right. He knew he wasn't home.

"Where —?" The word came out like a croak.

Someone heard him and came to his side. "Ned. Long Shanks."

He looked up and tried to focus on the face gazing down at him. "I — I know you. Jack ... Jack Frost."

"You're half right, son!" The man beamed and patted Ned's shoulder. "I'm Frosty Jack! Hear that, boys? He's coming around! Chilblains, you got the tea ready?" He propped Ned up and supported him while Chilblains held a hot drink to Ned's lips. "Drink this up. Come on, all of it!"

"Eughh!" Ned coughed and gagged as the bitter liquid went down his throat. "What the —?"

"Spruce needle tea," Frosty Jack said. "What you been calling juicy beetles. If you'd taken my advice in the first place, you wouldn't be in this sorry state. Early signs of scurvy, that's what you got, son. And a fever."

"Oh, no ..."

"Easy, now. We caught it in time. Caught *you* in time. Whatever were you thinking, stringing up that rope?"

"Don't remember ..."

Chilblains shook his head. "We said you could move in with us. When you first got here, that's what we said. The loneliness'll kill you, that's what we said. Just like it did ol' Mosquito. Ain't that right, Skipper?"

"That's right. But remember, Long Shanks? You said the dog'd keep you comp'ny. And sure 'nough it did. Saved yer life, that dog. If Mosquito'd had a dog —"

"Mosquito?" Ned frowned.

"The miner that built this cabin. Hung himself last winter. Round about the same time, too. Gosh sakes, we told you about that! Told you we reckoned the place might be haunted. Just pullin' yer leg, though. No hard feelings, eh? Gosh, if it hadn't been —"

"That's enough talk," Frosty Jack interrupted. "Let the lad rest." He turned his attention to Ned. "The boys'll take turns staying with you 'til you're on the mend. We're ready to take you to Dawson if need be, but that hospital's overcrowded as it is. Looks like your food supplies are holding up, but you're eating like a bird. No wonder you took sick."

"I tried. I got the sourdough starter like you said, but ... but at the end of the day ..."

"Save your strength, son. The missus'll be around with some sourdough bread and dried fruit, as soon as you're up to it."

Ned reached out a hand as if groping for something. "Nugget. Where's Nugget?"

At the sound of his name, Nugget gave a whoof and bounded to Ned's side.

"There's someone likes you, that's for sure." Frosty

Jack smiled, then looked skyward. "Someone up there likes you, too. You were that close to being a goner."

"What —" Ned struggled to remember.

"Don't you worry," said Skipper. "We'll fill you in later. First you gotta get yer strength back."

"I'm not home ..." Ned murmured. "I'm still here." He threw his arms around Nugget and sighed deeply. Whether it was a sigh of relief or disappointment, no one could say.

• • •

It was three weeks before Ned felt more like himself. By then he had drunk enough spruce needle tea to last a lifetime. At least they'd caught the scurvy in time. His gums hadn't started to bleed, no teeth had fallen out, and his legs were no longer in pain.

He learned that he'd been delirious the night the men found him, but he hadn't imagined the harness bells. Nugget had heard them, too, and while Ned was attempting to kick over the crates, the dog had raced outside.

"Came flyin' across the snow like a banshee!" Skipper told him. "Me 'n' Chilblains had the dog team, see, and we was off to meet Frosty with supplies. And that dog of yers, he was barkin' fit to be tied."

"It wasn't just that," Frosty Jack added. "I seen your cabin door wide open even before I took notice of the dog. That's a sure sign something's amiss. Weather like this, no one leaves a door wide open."

"I'll never be able to thank you," Ned said. "All of

you." His throat swelled up with emotion.

"Hey, it wasn't just us and the dog," Chilblains re-marked. "You got them long legs to thank, too. And the low cabin. You was half-conscious and ravin' with delirium, but that woulda been the fever. Sure, you got a sore throat from the rope burn, but if yer really set on that kind o' rope trick, you got to find yourself a higher beam."

Ned gave a wry smile. "Is that a nice way of saying I botched it?"

"Reckon so," said Frosty Jack. "We're glad you failed, least in that department. And I reckon you got a coupla loved ones at home who'd say exactly the same thing."

. 16 .

"That Dark-haired Girl ..."

"Hurry, hurry, hurry...!"

From one end of the beach to the other the cry was the same, as stampeders scrambled to find their goods before the tide came in and washed them out to sea. A wall had risen on the sand, a tottering wall of several hundred jumbled-up outfits.

Catherine was lucky. She'd no sooner jumped out of the scow than she'd spotted her outfit a few yards away. Better yet, her belongings were all in one place, not hurled about in a chaotic mess. And they were dry. There were no shredded bags or ruined sacks of flour. Not yet.

Quickly she strapped the first load of goods to her sled and hauled them to a spot above the high-water line. Then she hurried back for a second load.

As she was reloading her sled, she noticed the young girl she'd spoken to on the steamer. The ship had just entered the canal at the time, and the girl had squeezed in beside Catherine at the railing. Poor thing, it was clear she'd had a rough go of it. The look on her face, when that old-timer told her they still had another two weeks at sea. And the grateful smile, when Catherine said he was teasing.

It was harder to laugh away his next comment. They were staring at the snow-covered mountains, the leaden sky and the cold gray landscape, when Catherine felt the girl shiver. And the old buzzard had said, "Looks pretty grim, don't it? You can almost see the sign, 'Abandon hope, all ye cheechakos who enter here.'" As if anyone needed his discouraging words.

The girl had turned to Catherine and quietly asked, "What's a cheechako?"

Catherine had been about to say it meant a tenderfoot, or a newcomer. But either for the girl's sake or her own, she'd embellished the true meaning and said, "A cheechako is a very brave person. A person who triumphs over impossible odds."

Now it appeared the girl was facing the seemingly impossible task of finding her outfit. She ran desperately from one stack of goods to another, constantly tripping over sleds and dogs and people, with one eye fixed on the tide. It was already lapping the first line of the wall and spilling into bags and boxes.

Just then the man she was traveling with called out, "Sarah, come quick! I've found it!" But when the girl reached the outfit in question, she cried, "No, Mr. Waverley, no, that's not mine!" and continued her frantic search.

Catherine was dragging her fourth load when she

spotted a stack of crates and boxes, all labeled with the name *Sarah Turner*. That could well be the girl's outfit, she thought. She left her sled and found the girl near the tide line, picking through half-submerged sacks and sobbing with frustration. "Are you Sarah Turner?"

The girl nodded tearfully.

"Then your outfit's higher up the beach. I'll show you." She led Sarah to her belongings, shrugged off her thanks and resumed her own hauling.

A short time later, as Catherine was going back for her final load, she passed Sarah struggling up the beach with a sled stacked high with goods. She waved at Catherine, then turned to the older woman puffing at her side. "See that girl, Mrs. Waverley? That dark-haired girl? She's the one that found my outfit. I guess she heard Mr. Waverley calling my name."

Catherine smiled to herself when she overheard the woman's response. "What girl? Unless you mean that odd one over there. Hardly a girl, but no young lady, either. Not the way she's dressed. Imagine, a man's mackinaw and overalls. Disgraceful!"

It wasn't the first time Catherine had been criticized for the way she was dressed, and she knew it wouldn't be the last. She didn't care. She wanted to get the job done, that's all. And wearing a skirt was not the easiest way to do it. One only had to look at the other women, tripping over their long, cumbersome skirts, to know that.

Over the following weeks, as Catherine hauled her goods from one staging point to another, it crossed her mind that wearing a man's clothing might be attracting too much attention. But she steadfastly refused all offers of assistance, and ignored the jeering remarks made at her expense.

The girl, Sarah, was often just ahead of her on the trail, making her way as doggedly as Catherine. Why on earth was she going to the Klondike? Catherine wondered. Not that she cared. She'd spent sixteen years of her life learning not to care, and she wasn't about to start now.

Still, the girl was a puzzle. She kept looking over her shoulder and smiling at Catherine, as if Catherine needed encouragement. And one day Catherine overheard her ask her traveling companion if they could invite "that dark-haired girl" for supper.

"Absolutely not!" the older woman replied. "Really, Sarah. She's not the sort you'd want to associate with. You don't know the first thing about her."

"What sort is she, then? And how can we find out about her if we can't even talk to her?"

"No need to be impudent, young lady. One look tells you what sort she is. Off on her own, dressed like a heathen, face like a foreigner, men giving her the eye. I'll not hear another word about it. Supper, indeed."

Sarah had the last word. "She just looks lonely, Mrs. Waverley. That's how she looks to me."

Catherine frowned, bewildered and unexpectedly hurt by Sarah's words. Heathen, foreigner ... Neither was true, but that didn't bother her. She'd been called worse. But lonely? No! Just because she'd built a wall around herself didn't mean she was lonely. It meant she was smart. She had to be, to survive what she'd been through.

Later she became angry. "How dare she!" she muttered. "That chip of a girl, that Sarah! Out in the wilderness without any family that I can see. How dare she call me lonely!"

What made it worse was the way she'd said it. *Lonely ... That's how she looks to me ...* In a tone that wasn't so much pitying as concerned. As if she really cared.

It was a concept Catherine failed to understand. So she put it out of her mind and focused her attention on the trail. She still had a long, long way to go.

Chilkoot Pass

SPRING, 1898

. 17 .
Tragedy

Sarah stared up at the mountain, half-crazed with shock. The journey so far had been bad enough, but now? She couldn't be expected to climb that wall of ice and snow! It was perpendicular! And to do it with a fifty-pound pack on her back? Impossible! She had a good mind to dump everything and go straight back home. If it wasn't for that Ned!

An adventure, that's what he'd called it. Not a suicide mission. An adventure that would make them rich.

Gold, gold, gold. The kind she'd read about in fairy tales. But to reach the gold, the hero had to overcome obstacles and pass certain tests. And the latest test in this particular fairy tale was climbing that horrendous mountain.

What if she couldn't make it to the summit? What if she fell and hurt herself? So far, the trials she'd suffered on the journey had been as difficult as those in a fairy tale. But she'd yet to see any fairy godmothers or supernatural beings, eager to help at the whisk of a magic wand.

If only Mother were here ... Sarah swallowed back a sob. No use crying. She had to play the part of the hero. She had to be strong and courageous. Like that dark-haired girl said, she was a cheechako, a person who triumphed over impossible odds.

She'd made it this far. But it had truly been one wretched test after another.

The first had been the sea voyage. One week of cramped and smelly quarters, rain sloshing in through the portholes, rough seas, and heaving into a filthy bucket. There were days when she'd wished the steamer would strike a rock or run aground or sink — *anything* to stop the seasickness.

After that, there'd been three weeks of slogging through snow and slush on a crowded trail, hauling supplies from one base camp to the next. And her sled's runners getting bogged down at every turn, and her feet killing her, and Mrs. Waverley complaining and not packing her share of the load, and the men on the trail, grumpy and impatient, yelling curses whenever someone stopped to rest. And it snowed and it rained and it snowed and it was so thoroughly dreadful, Sarah muttered a few curses of her own. Quietly, though, so Mrs. Waverley wouldn't hear.

It was mostly men on the trail, but Mother had been right about more and more women getting gold-rush fever. Sarah had met one of them, a Mrs. Nickerson from Nova Scotia who was traveling with her husband and son, Thomas, a boy Sarah's age. And there was the dark-haired girl Mrs. Waverley didn't like. But there was no time to talk to anyone, or make friendships, not with everyone so in-tent on getting through the next ordeal. And so worn out once they'd done it.

The previous evening, as they were eating their usual supper of bacon and beans, Mr. Waverley had announced that the next day they'd be climbing to the summit of the Chilkoot Trail. "And as an incentive, when we've made the first trip, perhaps we could have that ham at tomorrow's supper?" He glanced longingly at the tinned ham poking out from one of the packs.

Mrs. Waverley had refused. "No, my dear, we're saving that ham for Easter. It won't be long now, and we'll be glad of something special to mark the occasion."

Remembering this, Sarah hoisted her heavy pack and wished Mrs. Waverley wasn't so stingy. The thought of a lovely baked ham right now was much more appealing than gold. That Ned! If it wasn't for him, she'd be home right now, enjoying a good hearty supper. And she'd be warm. And she wouldn't have fifty pounds strapped to her back. And she wouldn't have to climb that impossible mountain.

"It does look rather daunting, doesn't it?" Beside her, Mrs. Waverley was clearly having the same misgivings.

"Just think of it as one more little stage," Mr. Waverley said. "Are you ready? Let's give it our best shot."

Sarah gave a loud sigh, and followed the Waverleys into the line.

It wasn't long before she found herself bent double, not only from the weight of the pack, but also from the steepness of the grade. If she stood up straight she was certain she'd fall over backwards. Not that she'd fall very far. Not with the hundreds of stampeders trudging at her heels.

Up and up and up ... One foot in front of the other, as Father used to say. Slow and steady wins the race ...

She was slow and steady, all right, with her head fixed thoroughly in the clouds. Unlike her wild, impulsive brother who continually leaped from one outrageous idea to another. How exasperated Father used to get.

Well, on *this* stage of the journey Ned couldn't have speeded things up if he'd tried. A slow and steady lockstep was the only way.

After what seemed like hours, Sarah reached the first rest spot, an area sheltered by a gigantic boulder known as Stone House. After that, it was onward and upward to the second rest spot, the Scales. Everyone had to rest there. The flat ledge at the Scales was the last place to catch one's breath before the steepest and most grueling part of the climb — the Golden Stairs. It was the final push to the summit, a staircase of hundreds of steps carved out of the ice.

Sarah waited as the Waverleys stepped into line and began their ascent. Then it was her turn. She looked up and groaned. The thought of that climb ...

"Just take it one step at a time. Cheechako, remember?"

Sarah looked around and saw the dark-haired girl waiting to join the line. "A very brave person and impossible odds." She grinned. "You can go ahead if you want. I don't mind."

"I did it yesterday," the girl said as she slipped in front of Sarah. "It's hard. But at least there's a rope to hang on to."

Sarah nodded gamely. Urging herself to triumph over yet another obstacle, she grasped hold of the rope and began to climb. Up, up the Golden Stairs, one icy step at a time.

She ignored the stomach cramps, the falling snow, the ache in her back, her blistering feet. She tried not to think of the number of trips she'd have to make to haul up her whole outfit. Instead she thought of Ned. He would have climbed these very steps, packing a much heavier load. He would have made it to the summit. She would, too. But not easily. By the time she reached the top she was groaning as much as the rest of the stampeders, even those who looked the strongest.

Mr. Waverley, who'd insisted on packing one hundred pounds, looked quite the worse for wear. "That's it for today," he panted. "We'll cache our packs here."

The summit was a freight yard, thronging with people and animals. Mr. Waverley managed to find a clear spot amidst the staggering piles of goods and helped his wife and Sarah unload.

Mrs. Waverley moaned with exhaustion. "I can't go back, James. I can't do it again, not tomorrow. I simply can't ..."

"You have to!" Sarah's outburst surprised everyone, including herself. She apologized, then added, "You'll feel better after a rest. And some supper. As soon as we're back in camp I'll fire up the stove and bake some biscuits."

Mrs. Waverley groaned. "That filthy camp ... Oh, Lord. I can't go back, only to begin again and again and again. It's too much for my heart, James. We should have taken the White Pass route, I told you we should've. At least then we could've used a sled, and horses. Even a dog can't make it up here. Did you see that poor man carrying his dog up those dreadful stairs? If we'd taken —" She stopped short, and her tone changed abruptly. "Sarah! What on earth are you doing?"

While Mrs. Waverley was talking, Sarah had ducked behind a tall stack of goods and removed her petticoats. It was clear to her that the dark-haired girl in overalls was having a much easier time than any of the conventionally dressed women. "It's too hard to climb with all this on," she said. She crumpled up the petticoats and stashed them in her pack.

"Really, Sarah! What would your mother say?"

"She wouldn't like it," Sarah admitted. "But she's not here, and I'm the one that has to do the climbing."

Mrs. Waverley sighed, too worn out to argue.

"Come along, my dear," her husband said. "We'll have a good supper and a good night's sleep, and you'll feel better in the morning. It's all downhill from here."

Smiling at his joke, he led them to a chute at the side of the stairs, sat himself and his wife on two shovels, and off they went, sailing straight to the bottom.

Sarah tucked up her skirt and followed. It was a swift and exhilarating ride, the chute worn shoulder-deep and smooth by the thousands of stampeders using it every day. Five hours to climb up — and one minute to slide down. She couldn't help but cheer.

• • •

There were several days of fine weather at the end of March. Sarah was beginning to think of spring when suddenly, on the last day of the month, they were hit by a relentless snowstorm. For three days it raged, forcing everyone to remain in the camp. But on the fourth day, even though it was still snowing heavily, many stampeders were once again ready to face the summit.

Mr. Waverley was among them. "Nothing we haven't climbed through before," he said. "Come along, Sarah. You, too, my dear."

Mrs. Waverley had clearly been doing a great deal of thinking over the previous three days. As they were resting at Stone House she announced, "I'm going back home. And you, Sarah, you're coming with me. This is no place for a girl. No place for a woman. No place for a sensible man, if you want my opinion. We've all of us got dysentery, the wretched camp stinks of beans and bacon and unwashed bodies, the weather is — the weather —" She began to sob.

"Things will get better." Mr. Waverley patted her shoulder. "Stay back at the camp the next few days, give yourself a good long rest. I know it's been hard. But I promise —"

"No! I'm done with your promises, James Waverley! I'm done arguing, I'm going home. You go on if you like, find your gold, it doesn't matter to me. You hear, Sarah? Your mother, she was the lucky one, breaking her leg the way she did. Sparing herself all this misery. We'll explain, we'll tell her the truth of the matter. She'll understand. Dear Lord! Just look at this place! The snow's falling sideways! The wind, the cold — Ohh! I can't bear it!"

"Bertha, calm yourself. Listen, I'll pay the professional packers to carry the rest of your load. You won't need to lift a finger."

"It's too late, James! I'm telling you, and Sarah ..."

Sarah was no longer listening. She'd stepped back into line and was staggering up the trail, anxious to reach the summit — or at least the Scales — before the blizzard got worse. It was madness. She could barely see the climber in front of her. As for the Waverleys, they were completely lost from view.

Was it really the beginning of April? At home, the parks and gardens would be bright with orange and purple crocuses, yellow daffodils and wild Easter lilies. Mother would be at church, maybe this very minute, celebrating Palm Sunday. Sarah felt a tug at her heart, knowing she would be in her mother's prayers.

Up and up and up ... Almost there. A few more steps ... At last she reached the Scales. She dropped her pack and rubbed her aching shoulders, wondering what to do next. Continue to the summit? Wait for the Waverleys? Slide down right here and now? All around her, people were asking the same question.

She thought she heard the voice of the boy from Nova Scotia. "Thomas?" she said. She could make out forms, but not features. With scarves wrapped up to the eyes, and hats pulled over the foreheads, faces were unrecognizable.

"Thomas!" She spoke more loudly, and this time a figure turned and stepped toward her.

"That you, Sarah? I'm climbing on up. My folks are there already. Do you want to go ahead?"

"No, I'm going back down. It's — No, wait." The thought that the climb she'd just endured might have been for nothing convinced her. "I'll go ahead. Thanks."

Up and up and up ... Finally she reached the summit. She had no sooner done so than she heard a deafening, heart-stopping roar. She froze, terrified. Before she could ask what was happening, another roar engulfed the mountains.

An eerie silence followed. Then all at once people began to cry out, "Oh God! It's an avalanche!"

"Where? Over the camp?"

"Sounds closer to the Scales ..."

"Came down Long Hill ..."

"Oh no. Dear God, all those people ..."

Sarah stumbled to the Waverleys' cache. People were moving like ghostly apparitions, stunned by what had happened. "It came down between the camp and the Scales," someone said. "Anyone on the hill got buried for sure."

"Sarah, you all right?"

She looked up, realized she'd been holding her breath and let it out in a gasp. "Oh, Thomas, the Waverleys! What if, what if — if they were still on the hill —" Her body shook with fear.

Thomas' mother appeared just then and took her in her arms. "No one knows anything yet, dear. It's too soon to say."

"Mrs. Waverley — she, she wanted to go back down," Sarah stammered. "When I left them at Stone House, she said, she said she wasn't going any farther. So — so they were probably well away from the hill when the avalanche — Don't you think?"

"I think there's a very good chance they're safe in

their tent. Let's go see, shall we? Come along."

Sarah allowed herself to be led down to the camp, praying the Waverleys would be safe. But their tent was empty.

"You can wait in our tent if you like," Thomas said.

Sarah thanked him but declined. She'd get the fire going and heat up some yellow pea soup for when the Waverleys got back. Mrs. Waverley would be happy to find the tent warmed up, and a hot supper ready that wasn't beans.

Once that was done, Sarah left the soup simmering on the stove and went outside to see if she could find the Waverleys in the crowded camp. If they hadn't come back after Sarah left them, then they must have continued on up to the summit. The chute was untouched by the avalanche. Perhaps they were sliding down right now. But there was no sign of the Waverleys at the base of the chute, or anywhere else in the area.

As she was returning to the tent, she passed Thomas and his father. Both were armed with shovels.

"Any luck?" Thomas asked.

"No ..." Sarah bit her lip to keep it from trembling.

"Chin up, lass," Mr. Nickerson said. "There's hundreds of digging crews on the hill."

"We'll look out for you, Sarah." Thomas gave her an encouraging smile. "There's people being found that were buried over twenty feet deep. And they're still alive. So don't worry."

Sarah couldn't help but worry. And when the Waverleys failed to return that night or the next day, she began to lose hope.

On the third day, Mrs. Nickerson came with the dreaded news. "They found their bodies, Sarah. I'm so sorry."

"But — but they were going to go back! Mrs. Waverley didn't want to climb another step!"

"She must have changed her mind. We'll never know why. The sad thing is, from what we've heard, everyone on the hill was on their way down when the avalanche happened. They could see how grim it was in that blizzard, and they were all hanging on to a rope to help them down."

Sarah burst into tears. "The ham!" she cried. "We should've eaten the tinned ham! But Mrs. Waverley, she was saving it for Easter. I know I shouldn't be thinking of that, but Mr. Waverley, you should've seen how his eyes lit up when he spotted that ham. That's all I can think — that ham, and how badly he wanted it. I — I can't stop shaking!"

"You're in shock." Mrs. Nickerson wrapped a blanket around Sarah and held her. "It's a terrible tragedy, terrible. And you being on your own ..." She paused for a moment. "You're welcome to travel with us. We'll see that you get to the Klondike safely, unless you decide to go home. And if that's the case, we'll find you a suitable traveling companion. Goodness knows, there's plenty turning back now. But you sleep on it, Sarah. Let me know in the morning."

All night long Sarah argued with herself. The thought of being safe at home, away from the wilderness, the cruel weather, the endless crowds ... What wouldn't she give to be home?

But to turn back when she'd come this far? Mother was counting on her. She'd expect her to carry on. Wouldn't she?

No ... Mother would expect Ned to carry on. She'd expect Sarah to give up and go home.

And for that reason, to prove not only to her mother but to herself she had the courage to continue, Sarah made her decision. "I'll come with you," she announced the next day, and gave Mrs. Nickerson a determined smile.

. 18 .

A Good Omen

Catherine didn't know why she'd given the girl the eggs. She'd bought them for herself, as a reward for missing the avalanche. Sheer luck, that's all it was. Unbelievable luck, that up there on the hill she'd been holding on to the back end of the rope, while everyone holding on to the front end had been buried. Sheer luck. Or maybe it was Fate. Maybe for the first time in her life, Fate had looked her way and smiled.

If that wasn't reason enough, she'd bought those three precious eggs as a treat for Easter Sunday. She certainly hadn't meant to give them away.

But as she was passing by the Nickerson tent, she heard Sarah say, "Here's a tinned ham, Mrs. Nickerson. Mrs. Waverley wanted it saved for Easter. I think she'd be pleased if, if we —" Her voice broke.

Mrs. Nickerson gave her a hug. "How kind, Sarah. It'll be some treat. Thank you."

Before Catherine knew it, she was offering her eggs to Sarah. "Here, take these," she said. "I'm sorry for your loss." With that, she hurried away.

She heard Mrs. Nickerson calling after her, "Wait, Miss! You'll join us for supper, won't you? Sarah, go after her."

"Wait! Please stay!" Sarah cried.

Before she could catch up, Catherine had lost herself in the crowd.

Why didn't you accept their invitation? In the days that followed, Catherine asked herself that question many times. And the answer was always the same.

Why? Because I don't want to know anyone, or speak to anyone, or answer any questions about who I am or where I've come from. And I especially don't want to be with people who feel sorry for me because they think I'm lonely. I'm not lonely. I don't even know what it means. The girl on the island, she might have known. But I don't.

The rigorous journey had done wonders in blocking out the memory of the girl she'd left behind. By the end of the day Catherine was too exhausted to think, let alone worry about what she'd done. Sleep came easily. But so did the nightmare.

In spite of the distance it crept into her sleeping mind and bludgeoned it with the past. *Look, Catherine. See that girl? See what she did?*

She hadn't meant to do it. Or had she? When the nightmare welled up in the dark and the walls of the island closed in, she'd wake up and scream, *Yes! Yes, I meant to do it! And I'm glad, I'm glad!*

She convinced herself that the nightmare was brought on by the cold. By the strangeness of the land. By physical exhaustion. By the constant crush of people. Once she reached the end of the journey, the nightmare would surely end.

As she looked at the faces of her fellow stampeders, she saw any number of sorrows and worries and fears. She realized they were all suffering from one nightmare or another. And for many, the most horrendous nightmare of all was clearly the journey itself.

• • •

The week following Easter brought several days of fine weather, then three solid days of blizzards. In spite of the wind and blowing snow, Catherine's spirits were high. They were nearing the end. Only three more climbs to the summit. Then two. Then one.

It was near the end of April when she made her last agonizing climb, and as luck would have it, the moment she reached the summit the sky cleared. She took it as a good omen, another example of Fate smiling her way.

There was one more hurdle before the Chilkoot stage of the journey was over. Since the stampeders were about to cross into Canadian territory, the North West Mounted Police had raised the Union Jack and set up a customs post. No one could proceed unless they had a year's worth of supplies. And if their goods hadn't been bought in Canada, they had to pay the necessary customs duties.

As usual, there was an interminable lineup. Catherine

hauled the last of her goods into line, and somehow found herself in the middle of the Nickerson group.

"Are you traveling with this party, Miss?" the constable asked when Catherine's turn came.

The question took her by surprise. She was about to say she was traveling alone when Mrs. Nickerson spoke up. "She is indeed traveling with us. And her name —" She raised her eyebrows in a question.

"Catherine," she replied.

The constable wrote it down. "And your last name?"

Catherine froze. It was a trap. The Seattle police had put out a notice and now the Canadian police were watching for her. If she gave her real name —

"It's not a difficult question," the constable said. "Just need it for our records. Come on, the stampede's still on, you know. There's thousands waiting behind you."

She said the first word that came to mind. "Rush. Catherine Rush." Then she smiled. The name was perfect. Every step on the trail, through ice and snow and slush and mud, every step was rushing her away from the girl on the island. Soon she would be free.

. 19 .
Break-up

At the end of May, Sarah was awakened by a low rumbling crack, as loud as a gunshot. She cried out in alarm, terrified it might be another avalanche. But that couldn't be. They were at Lake Bennett, well away from the avalanche zone.

She heard the crack again. This time it was followed by several loud, boisterous cheers. A smile spread across her face as she realized what it was. The ice on the lake was breaking.

She leapt out of her sleeping bag, got dressed and raced outside to join the excited crowd.

Mr. Nickerson greeted her on the shore. "You heard it, too, eh? Won't be long now. Before you know it, that lake'll be clear and we'll be off."

"Oh, I hope so!" she said. She was certain the worst was over. In fact, ever since they'd arrived at Lake Bennett things had been easier. The trip down from the summit had been a breeze. With sails rigged up to their sleds, the wind did the work. They only had to follow along. And the weather had turned fine, although the sunlight glaring off the snow had been hard on the eyes. But it wasn't long before the warmth melted away the snow.

Spring had arrived in spite of the ice still holding on the lake. Wildflowers appeared on the hillside, creating patches of pink and yellow and blue against the melting snow. Clouds of ducks and geese filled the sky. Venturing into the woods to pick wild strawberries one day, Sarah came upon a grouse with chicks. And in a rare moment of relative quiet, she heard the familiar song of the robin.

The camp at Lake Bennett had been a shock at first, a huge conglomeration of tents and buildings and people and dogs. There were tent hotels and restaurants and dance halls, packed in with privies, chapels, casinos, even a tent post office. Warehouses and stores jostled for space along with wooden buildings and numerous log cabins.

A ragged stream of traffic flowed constantly amidst stacks of hay bales, sacks of flour, piles of green lumber and the hulls of partly constructed boats. And the noise! Short-tempered stampeders haggled for prices on precious items like nails or pitch or additional feed. Dogs yelped and barked and snarled. Saws screeched, hammers pounded, trees crashed to the ground.

With the lengthening hours of daylight, men worked day and night, falling trees, whipsawing the trunks, then bashing the boards into some kind of boat.

While Mr. Nickerson and Thomas worked on their boat, Sarah helped Mrs. Nickerson and Catherine wash clothes and cook the meals. She even made an apple pie one day, using some of the dried apples her mother had packed, with a few wild strawberries thrown in. Since there was no rolling pin, she used a baking powder can to roll out the pastry. And since there was no proper cake board, she used the top of her grub box, covered with a cloth. Sprinkled with cinnamon, baked in the Yukon stove, the pie came out browned to a turn.

"Best apple pie I've ever eaten," Thomas said when he'd finished his second piece.

Sarah blushed with pride. It was the first time she'd ever received a compliment on her baking.

By the middle of May, Mr. Nickerson had finished the boat. Seams had been caulked and pitched, and the mast was fitted to the beam.

"It's a fine-looking boat," Sarah said.

Mr. Nickerson looked up from the pair of oars he was making. "Oh, we've built a boat or two where we come from," he remarked. "I could give most of these fellows a bit of advice, but they're in too much of a hurry to listen. Think they know it all. But we know different."

Sarah grinned. She'd heard more than one stampeder tell Mr. Nickerson that, if they could pack two thousand pounds over the blasted pass, they could build a little boat, thank you very much.

Later, Thomas had taken Sarah aside and said, "I'll tell you a secret. My dad never built a boat in his life."

"You're joking!"

"Nope, he's just counting on his Nova Scotia blood, something he hopes our boat-building ancestors passed on through the genes. That, and a lot of luck. So keep your fingers crossed."

Sarah had promised that she would.

Now that the ice had broken, an even greater sense of urgency prevailed. Men worked harder than ever. Every hour saw more ice pans floating down the lake. Some stampeders, unable to wait another second, were already starting out.

Two days later, the lake was clear of ice. Over eight hundred boats were ready to leave for Dawson, the advance guard for the thousands to follow. The atmosphere became less frenzied and more like a carnival as shouts of good wishes and a fusillade of rifle shots saw the boats on their way.

The *Ella Jane* was amongst them. When Mr. Nickerson was satisfied that she rode an even keel with no sign of any leaks, they loaded their goods and set sail on the last stage of the journey.

. 20 .
Becalmed

Catherine stared across the glassy green surface of the lake. The gusty wind that had sent the *Ella Jane* skimming over the water had died down, and now the boat was becalmed.

"No sense rowing," Mr. Nickerson said. "The wind'll pick up before long. We'll take advantage of the lull, have a bit of a breather."

Catherine leaned on the oar and waited for the wind.

The whole flotilla was becalmed. Boats of all shapes and sizes had set out from Bennett that morning, from flat-bottomed skiffs like the *Ella Jane* to tiny craft that looked more like children's toys than seaworthy vessels. Scows, barges, rafts, canoes — they formed a line at least three miles long.

In every boat there was a person — stampeder, gold seeker, dreamer, fool. Every one of them had a secret, something left behind. Becalmed, certainly. But never calm.

Catherine watched as they washed their socks, mended their shirts, smoked their pipes. They strummed banjos, played mouth organs, whistled or sang. Many sat quietly, contemplating the scene around them. Perhaps anticipating what lay ahead. Or trying to forget what they'd left behind.

It wasn't easy to forget. The dugout canoe floating alongside the *Ella Jane* reminded Catherine of another canoe. The girl had escaped in that canoe, then pushed it back out to sea.

The owner is missing, they would say when they found it. Missing and presumed drowned. Gone without a trace.

She trailed her fingers in the water, waiting for the wind.

The night she'd left the island had been a windless night. She had paddled hard, every stroke beating back the memory of what she was leaving behind. Gone, gone, her paddle sang. Away with that life, away with that girl, and on to a new beginning.

Rush, rush ... She had flown across the water.

But now ... Oh, how she wished for a wind.

She was so absorbed in her thinking she hadn't noticed that Sarah had sat down beside her. "I'm glad you joined us," Sarah said. "I wanted you to, right from the beginning, when I was with the Waverleys. But Mrs. Waverley ... Well, it wasn't that she was unkind, she just had this notion ..."

"It doesn't matter." Catherine turned her attention back to the water. She wished the wind would come and rustle things up. The stillness was unsettling, especially after so much activity.

Sarah spoke again. "Is this journey what you expected?"

"Yes and no," Catherine replied. Then, before Sarah could ask another question, she asked one of her own. "What's the first thing you'll do when you get to the Klondike?"

"That's easy! First I'm going to find my brother, the one I told you about. He's wonderful, Ned is. He's handsome and lively and very clever. He was planning to go to the university. Only Father died, that was two years ago, and left us a bit desperate. Ned quit school, he was fourteen, and got a job. He gave all his earnings to Mother. And she had to work, taking in laundry and sewing and that sort of thing. It was hard, never knowing from one month to the next if we'd be able to pay the bills." She laughed. "Listen to me, I sound just like my mother! That's all changed now. When I find Ned, we'll go home as rich as the Klondike kings."

Catherine raised an eyebrow and gave her a skeptical look.

"It's true!" Sarah exclaimed. "You must believe it, otherwise you wouldn't be here. Or maybe — I'm sorry. I should've asked you sooner. Do you have a brother or somebody you want to find? Is that why you're going?"

Catherine turned away without answering. There was no one she wanted to find. No one in the world. Maybe that's what was meant by lonely.

. 21 .

Thousands Upon Thousands

Once the initial lull was over, the days flew by with fine, windy weather. Every night the Nickerson party made camp to eat, and after catching a few hours' sleep, they were once again on the water.

A river-way that turned into a swirling roll of mud took them from Lake Bennett into Tagish Lake. There the Mounted Police checked the boats and asked for customs receipts. They also warned the stampeders to be careful.

Keep a sharp lookout! The cry was passed from one boat to another. No one knew what was coming. Fallen timber? Boulders? Sharp, unexpected bends?

Sarah kept watch with the others, ready to shout at the first sign of a jutting rock or a floating log. She wasn't expecting to be swept into a canyon and engulfed in the roar of rushing waters. Before she knew it, the *Ella Jane* had plunged into a whirlpool, dropped several feet and risen up again. As she clutched her lurching stomach and fought for breath, the whirlpool grabbed hold of the boat, spun it around and tossed it out the other side.

The worst wasn't over. The river narrowed and hurled the boat down a twenty-foot drop, this time even more abrupt and dangerous than the previous plunge had been. Waves frothed and kicked upon the boulders like a herd of galloping horses.

Sarah clung to Catherine, desperate to be back on land or becalmed on the lake. Struggling up the Chilkoot in a blizzard was better than this.

"Dad's going with the current to stay clear of the rocks," Thomas shouted. "Don't worry, Sarah. He's spent his life on the sea."

"This isn't the sea!" she wailed. If they made it through the White Horse Rapids it would be a miracle.

As Thomas predicted, the *Ella Jane* followed the current and landed them in calmer waters. Mr. Nickerson was swamped with offers to pilot other boats through the rapids. Thirty, forty, fifty dollars — the desperate fellows would pay anything. But he refused. The slightest delay might mean he would miss the chance at the goldfields.

After another stretch of bubbling water, the boat was churned into Lake Laberge. "This is the last of the lakes," Thomas said as they were eating supper on the shore. "And it's the prettiest. One of the old-timers back at Bennett, he told me."

Sarah waved a hand in front of her face. "Did he tell you about the mosquitoes, too?"

The mosquitoes had been bad enough at Lake Bennett,

but now, as the days grew increasingly warmer, they were a terror. The shores of Lake Laberge were dotted with campfires made purposefully smoky to discourage the beasts. It didn't help.

Sarah had laughed when she heard that in the north, a mosquito could kill a dog or blind a bear. Or cover an animal in such thick swarms you couldn't see its hide.

She wasn't laughing now. She almost believed the tall tales about mosquitoes so big and fierce they stood in the water and speared the stampeders right out of their boats.

They soon discovered that netting was no protection, as the mosquitoes could force their way through. Thomas figured they worked in teams. "The way I see it, a couple of mosquitoes hold another one's legs tight to his body so he can get through the net, then it's another one's turn."

"I don't think so," his father said. "Those mozzies are way too ornery to work in teams."

Everyone took to wearing gloves and scarves to protect their hands and necks. Catherine solved the problem of protecting their faces. She took out the black tulle she'd brought from the tailor's shop, cut it into pieces and sewed each piece into a cylinder. She then attached two elastic bands, one for the top to fit over one's hat, the other at the bottom to go around the throat. Everyone looked odd, but it did the trick. Until it was time to eat.

At mealtime, the terrors were waiting. The instant the tulle was lifted up to free the mouth, in they swarmed.

"I give up!" Sarah finally said. "I'd rather go hungry." Her face was a mess of bites, not only from mosquitoes, but from blackflies and gnats. It was also blistered and burned from the twenty-odd hours of sunlight. If Ned were to see her now, he wouldn't even recognize her.

• • •

Lake Laberge emptied into yet another foaming stretch of water that spun their boat over half-submerged rocks. After that they were hurled through more rapids and whirlpools. Finally they reached the full stream of the Yukon River.

Down they went, some sixty miles a day, one boat in a flotilla of thousands. They stopped to eat, but no longer to sleep. There wasn't time. They were close. Everyone felt it.

Somewhere around the bend ...

On the right bank ...

Around the next bend, where the blue waters of the Klondike rushed into the silty Yukon —

And suddenly, there it was. Dawson City!

Sarah stared in awe. It was more than a city. It was a metropolis! A sprawling metropolis that stretched along the river and over the swamp and up the hillside — why, it was bigger than Victoria! And it wasn't a city of gold as she'd been led to believe. It was a city of mud, a swamp of gumbo so thick and deep she could see wagons stuck up to their wheel hubs, and horses straining to pull them free.

And the smell! Her nose wrinkled with the stench of garbage and sewage and manure drifting out to the river. If poor Mrs. Waverley had made it this far, she would've taken one sniff and caught the next boat home.

As for the noise! Sarah had thought the camp at Lake Bennett was noisy. Here, the very river rocked with the clamor of falling trees, pounding hammers and shrieking saws.

"Quite the place, eh?" Thomas stood beside her and looked out at the town.

"It's — it's —" Sarah let out her breath in a sigh. The thought of leaving the boat and stepping into that mess of a city was daunting. "It's not what I expected."

"We'll get used to it." Mrs. Nickerson squeezed her shoulder. "Have you ever seen so many people?"

"No ..." She had, of course. Since the journey began she'd been engulfed by an endless tide of people. But they'd always been on the move. Now they'd passed the final test and reached the end of the trail. She could see them milling aimlessly about the town, thousands upon thousands.

And along the river, more than two miles of boats were tied to the shore, their sides jammed up against each other. More boats were arriving by the minute. And clambering out of every skiff, scow, raft and barge, out of every punt and canoe, out of the steamboat arriving from the north, were more and more stampeders.

Sarah shuddered.

"Are you all right?" Thomas asked.

She shook her head, sick at heart. She'd come to the end of the journey. She'd finally reached the Klondike. But how would she ever find her brother?

. 22 .
I'm Trying Very Hard

June 19, 1898

Dear Mother,

I hope you are well. I'm fine. I've been in Dawson City a week now. I'm living with Mrs. Nickerson in a log cabin up the hill. There's no running water and no sewer but the owner garanteed it's free of lice and we have our own privy which is a luxury here.

Mrs. Nickerson invited Catherine to come and live here too. (Catherine's the girl I told you about in the letter I sent from Bennett.) But she's living somewhere else.

Sarah paused. Where was Catherine? The minute they'd arrived in Dawson, she'd unloaded her outfit and disappeared. Sarah was watching out for her, but the chances of finding anyone in Dawson were pretty slim. If someone wanted to get lost, this was surely the place. As for Ned ...

I haven't found Ned yet but I'm trying very hard. I think you will be surprized when you hear what I'm doing.

Will she even care? Sarah wondered. Or will she be angry that I haven't found him?

She continued with her letter.

I'm sure I'll find him soon. I'm meeting lots of people and asking everybody if they've seen him.

I hope your leg is better. I wish you were here. Mrs. Nickerson is really nice. (Her name is Ella Jane, and thats what they called there boat.) Thomas is nice too, and so is Mr. Nickerson. But there not here in Dawson there out at the goldfields to stake a claim. There going to look for Ned too.

I'll send another letter soon. (Not like Ned)

Heaps of love,
Sarah

She put the letter in an envelope, filled a basket with freshly baked bread and, after saying good-bye to Mrs. Nickerson, set off for her bread stand on Front Street.

As she made her way along the muddy street, still

steaming after the morning's rain, Sarah couldn't help but think, If only Mother could see me now! She may have been discouraged when she first arrived in Dawson, but in the days that followed she had not been idle. The dreamer that had once driven her mother to distraction had been replaced by a doer of great strength and resourcefulness. At least, that's how she saw herself now. If anyone could find Ned, she could.

She had first inquired at the gold commissioner's office. After all, Ned had come to find gold so he must have staked a claim. But there was no record of him there.

Next, she'd gone to the North West Mounted Police post. "Ned Turner's the name?" a Corporal Murdoch asked. "First we'll see if he's on the woodpile list."

"He might have worked on the woodpile," Sarah said. "He's always eager to lend a hand."

The corporal laughed. "Here in Dawson, you don't volunteer to work on the woodpile. It's what serves as a jail. Two or three days chopping wood, especially when it gets to forty-five below — that makes any man think twice before committing a crime."

Sarah looked affronted. "Then he definitely won't be on that list."

All the same, Corporal Murdoch scanned the names. Then, satisfied, he closed the book. "You could check the hospital. After that, your best bet is to put a notice on the corner of the Alaska Commercial, that big log building on Front Street. Everyone coming in or going out of Dawson checks there for messages."

Sarah went to the hospital, and when that proved

fruitless, she posted a sign on the Alaska Commercial notice board.

> *If anyone knows the whereabouts of Ned Turner please*
> *contact Sarah at the Nickersons log cabin five streets up*
> *from here and two over. It's two doors south of where all the*
> *dogs are. Including the black lab with three legs.*

There were so many cabins with so many dogs, she hoped Ned would find the right one. She hoped he'd see the message amongst the hundreds of others tacked to the board. But if he didn't, maybe a friend would, or a partner.

She had also tacked up a message for Catherine, in case she changed her mind and wanted to stay with the Nickersons.

That taken care of, she had walked up and down Front Street, hoping one of the men she passed might be her Ned.

At first glance, they all looked the same, dressed in worn-out mackinaws, high boots, tattered trousers, wide-brimmed hats. She thought of Ned's portrait, how he'd posed in his new Klondike garb. How many of these men had done the same? She examined every face, hoping Ned might spring out from the dirty, unkempt beards.

If she failed to recognize him, he couldn't help but notice her. There were few women about, and even fewer children. Her very presence on the crowded street attracted attention, and all of it was friendly. Men smiled, tipped their hats, stepped aside so she could pass more easily and asked if she needed a hand.

"I'm looking for my brother, Ned Turner," she told them. "Do you know him?"

"Nope, never heard that name," they said.

"Trouble is," someone pointed out, "nobody here goes by their real name. Everybody ends up with a nickname. Back on the trail, there were dozens of men who traveled together for months and never learned each other's names. You take a look at the notice board, you'll see what I mean."

The man was right. When Sarah looked again, she saw names like Evaporated Kid, Oatmeal, Chilblains ... She should've known. It wasn't as if she hadn't been on the trail herself.

She had a similar problem when she described what Ned looked like — at least, the way he'd looked when he left for the Klondike.

"Fellas goin' by that description," everyone said, "they're a dime a dozen up here."

Then, often as not, they would add, "My, you look a picture, Miss. Just like my little girl back home."

It soon became obvious that many of the stampeders were giving up. They were selling off the goods they'd carried and dragged across mountains and down rivers, and hoping to get enough money so they could pay for their passage home. Everything was for sale, from long johns to satin slippers, from mining gear to food supplies. A man turning back didn't need a pick or shovel or gold pan. Nor did he need five hundred pounds of flour, two hundred pounds of bacon or one hundred pounds of beans.

A few smart fellows were making a fortune selling what nobody else had thought to bring. Sarah wished she had something to sell, something the miners might need or want. She could set up a stand, earn a bit of money and ask about Ned at the same time.

It was then she'd come up with the idea of a bread stand. Freshly baked bread — why, those miners would catch one whiff and the bread would go like hotcakes.

She had hurried back to the cabin, eager to discuss her idea, and discovered that Mrs. Nickerson had a plan of her own. "How about a partnership, Sarah? I'll do the baking, you do the selling, and we'll split the proceeds. I'm also planning to do washing for the miners who come in from the creeks. I'll wash their shirts and trousers and then — and this can be your job — then you can pan the wash water."

"What for?" Had Mrs. Nickerson lost her head?

"For gold dust, my dear! Dust that brushes off a man's fingers and gets trapped in his cuffs and pockets. It washes out when you do the laundry. Between the two of us, we'll be in clover in no time."

Now, a week later, both plans were working well. As Sarah sold her last loaf of the day, she couldn't help but feel proud. Her poke was growing heavy with gold dust, and she'd made friends and contacts throughout the town.

"Say, Miss, I've a proposal." The miner who had just bought the bread was looking at the letter in Sarah's hand. "That is, if you're headin' for the post office?"

"I am, as a matter of fact," Sarah said. "I've got to buy a stamp and mail this. I have to hurry, too, before they open the doors for people to pick up their mail. There's such a lineup."

The miner agreed. "A bunch of mail sacks came in this morning. And another forty tons is on the way, from what I hear. And that brings me to my proposal. Joel Harris is the name. I'll pay you one ounce of gold, the going rate for standers, and another if you can find my letters. 'Course it'd mean standing in line for five or six hours, and another hour to look through the sacks. Those clerks in there, they've given up trying to sort. So whaddya say? I'd as soon pay you as someone else. And I got too many other things to do before I head back to the creeks."

"Sure, Mr. Harris. I'll do it." Sarah shook his hand, little knowing that her new job would eventually lead to her brother. But not in the way she expected.

. 23 .

She's Worth Her Weight in Gold

Catherine was dancing when she heard the voice.

Somehow it burst through the noise of the dance hall. Through the scraping violins, the thumping piano, the spirited shouts of the miners and the high-pitched laughter of the girls.

Somehow it made its way through and stopped her cold.

It couldn't be.

"Come along, Sweet Pea! I paid a dollar for this dance!" Her partner's arms tightened around her as he picked up the beat and whipped her around the floor.

It couldn't be.

Catherine told herself it was only the nightmare, hounding her even when she was awake. Not that she was ever asleep. It was daylight forever, even at night when she was working. And during the day it was impossible to sleep because of the constant noise.

The smoke in the dance hall made everything dream-like. The hanging oil lamps flickered and swayed. Girls whirled past in shimmers of gingham or faded silk. Miners drifted by in denim shirts and duck trousers. Those who weren't dancing stood at the side, watching, smoking, watching ...

Had the husky voice come from one of the watchers? If so — She stumbled, and lowered her head against her partner's chest.

Heel-and-Toe Eddy, so-called because of his fancy footwork on the dance floor, was a regular at the Davenport, but since Catherine had arrived, he'd danced only with her. "Don't fall asleep on me now, Sweet Pea!" he said. "What you need is a drink to perk you up."

Catherine forced a smile. Be lively and pleasant, the other girls had advised her. Then the miners spend more money at the bar. And the more money they spend, the more you get.

Catherine soon learned that that was exactly how it worked. One circuit of the dance hall, then off to the bar. The miner buys a couple of drinks and the girl gets a percentage.

"What's it to be tonight?" Heel-and-Toe asked.

Catherine caught the eye of the owner across the bar and saw him mouth the word *champagne*.

She quickly said, "Ginger ale," and ignored his scowl. Both she and the Davenport made more money if she ordered expensive drinks, but it was too underhanded for her liking. The miners were so desperate for a good time when they came to town, they'd pay anything, those who had the gold. Even those who didn't. After every dance they crowded the bar and slapped down their soft leather pokes.

A loud ruckus coming from the gambling room drew her attention away from the bar. Had the dreaded voice come from there? Would she hear it again?

No, because she hadn't heard it the first time. It was her imagination, that's all. The weariness, the noise ...

What was she doing here? She should've accepted Mrs. Nickerson's invitation. Just because she was getting attached to Sarah and the Nickersons, was that a reason to shy away? But it was so unexpected, that feeling of attachment. And somehow frightening, not knowing how to accept it.

Heel-and-Toe Eddy nudged her elbow. "Sweet Pea, you're way too serious. How about another dance?"

There were several more dances. Waltzes and polkas and two-steps. Then, after one frenzied waltz, Heel-and-Toe Eddy astounded Catherine with a proposition.

"What?" She couldn't have heard him right. She leaned against the bar, suddenly dizzy. Her head was spinning, and her stomach reeled.

"I got a good claim," he said, "and a log cabin. How 'bout you comin' out for a week? You can do some cookin' and washin' and what-not. And in return, unless you decide to marry me — heck, even if you do! — in return I'll give you your weight in gold. How much do you weigh, Sweet Pea? Not much more 'n a hundred pounds, I figure. So think of it, one hundred pounds o' gold!"

Catherine was speechless. The room swayed, and she gripped the edge of the bar to keep from falling.

A door opened in her mind, revealing another dark, smoke-filled room. A voice was saying, *You can take the girl and we'll call it square.* And the husky voice, *You got a deal! She's worth her weight in gold.*

The voices in her mind, the voice she'd heard earlier — it couldn't be him. He was dead. The girl on the island had killed him ...

"Well, Sweet Pea? Whaddya say?"

Catherine slammed the door on the nightmare. "No! How dare you! I'm worth more than that."

"We'll double it, then. Let's say two weeks, and we'll double your weight in gold. Hey, now! Don't walk away! At least gimme another dance!"

The band started playing. *There'll be a hot time in the old town tonight ...* The dancers sang, the watchers stamped their moccasined feet. Several miners approached Catherine as she made her way out of the dance hall, but she didn't stop.

Outside, it was as bright as day. Catherine went straight to the Alaska Commercial building, studied the notice board and eventually spotted the message she was hoping to find. Then she went back to the Davenport, slipped upstairs to her room and gathered up some of her belongings. The rest, she'd return for later.

Five streets up and two over ... The cabin wouldn't be hard to find, especially with the mention of the three-legged dog.

She hoped it wasn't too late, that Sarah and the Nickersons would still want her. But she needn't have worried.

"If you're not the answer to our prayers!" Mrs. Nickerson greeted her warmly. "But before I get into that, let's have a look at you! My goodness, it's the first time we've seen you in a dress. And what a picture!"

Catherine blushed. "I made it myself. For the dance hall."

"It suits you to a T. Doesn't it, Sarah? The next time we need a new dress we'll know who to come to. Now, sit yourself down. We've just finished breakfast. Are you hungry? No? Well, have some coffee at least and let me tell you what's happened. You see, Catherine, Mr. Nickerson has staked a claim and built us a cabin. Too Much Gold, the creek's called, although he says a better name might be Too Much Work." She went on to explain that she was anxious to move out of town and join her family, but refused to leave Sarah on her own.

Sarah was equally determined to stay. She was certain that Dawson was the place to find Ned, not some faraway creek. Sooner or later, someone would show up who knew him.

Mrs. Nickerson had finally given up trying to convince her. She'd been in the process of looking for someone to take Sarah in when Catherine appeared. "This here's a good solid cabin," she went on. "There's plenty of room for the two of you. I've paid up the next month's rent, don't you worry about that, and I'll explain about the laundry if you want to take over. It's a fine business, Sarah'll vouch for that. And the bread-making. Of course, it's up to you. You're a sensible young woman, Catherine Rush. I know that from those weeks on the trail. And you're hard-working and honest. Otherwise I wouldn't think of leaving Sarah with you. Now, let's give you the tour. It won't take but a minute, and you can let me know what you think."

Sarah reached out and clasped Catherine's hands. "Please say you'll stay."

"Mrs. Nickerson, Sarah ..." Her eyes brightened with tears. "Of course I'll stay." She promised herself she'd work hard. And she'd stay away from the dance halls, where the nightmare lurked and dragged her into the past.

SUMMER, 1898

. 24 .

Hot Time in the Old Town

Late June, 1898

*Another day washing the dumps. Hot. Flies fit to kill. The
sound of birds is a treat, when you can hear them through
the band-saw hum of a thousand mosquitoes. Frosty Jack
paid me up, so first chance I get I'm heading into Dawson ...*

It was early July when Ned set out for Dawson, his poke
bulging with the gold he'd saved after seven months of
hard labor. "$1,400!" he told Nugget. "Would've been more
if the cold hadn't slowed things down and if I hadn't got
sick. It's not a fortune, I know, but Mother can pay off the
mortgage and still have money to spare. Whaddya think?"

Nugget yapped excitedly.

Ned was optimistic. They were now washing the
dumps at Frosty Jack's, and with the long days he could
work longer hours. By August he'd be searching for a

claim of his own. As for going home? The truth was, he was starting to like the place.

He liked the vastness of the land and the trials it put a man through. To sink as low as you could get, and survive, and be the better for it — that was something to be proud of. As for the folks on the creeks, a more giving lot he'd be sore pressed to find. Any hint of misfortune or trouble, they were right there, willing to lend a hand. Of course, with the elements being what they were, and the remoteness, folks had to stick together.

And now, with the light — gosh almighty, it was something! The sun rose shortly after midnight, climbed until noon, then sank until it dipped below the horizon. Even then the sky remained bright and pale, with day merging into night so softly you scarcely noticed.

True, he hadn't struck it rich. But maybe this whole journey hadn't been about finding gold. Maybe it was the journey itself that was important, and what he'd discovered about himself.

As he walked the fifteen miles to Dawson, he marveled at what a difference a little time could make. Frosty Jack had been right way back in February, when he'd told Ned to hang on, to look at the good instead of the bad. The worst of the winter was over, he'd said. It would still be bitter cold — he was right about that — but every day would bring a few more minutes of light.

Ned smiled, remembering the eagerness with which he and the other miners had climbed the hills back in late February and early March, hoping to see the sun hovering on the horizon. And the shared jubilation when at last they'd seen the red ball of fire blazing against the cold blue sky.

By the end of April, beneath the thick layer of ice on the creeks, water had begun to flow. Ned remembered the exhilaration he'd felt on hearing that unmistakeable gurgle. And the pride when Frosty Jack slapped him on the back and said, "You made it, Long Shanks! You come up here a cheechako, but by God, you're a sourdough now!"

• • •

Eight months had passed since Ned had last been in Dawson, and he was amazed at the changes. "Just look at the place!" he exclaimed. "There's streets and houses and boardwalks, and hundreds of stores! It's a real city!"

The town was swarming with people, and everyone was trying to make the most of it. Every third door along Front Street was a saloon. Every saloon had a show for the price of a drink. And after every show there was dancing at a dollar a dance. "Nope," Ned muttered to himself. "Don't think so. On the other hand, Nugget ..." He thought for a moment. "Nope. We didn't come all this way to sashay in our gumboots. All the same ..."

He stopped to watch two young women singing on the boardwalk. A crowd had gathered to watch, and it wasn't long before the performers were collecting handfuls of glittering nuggets. When their little dog circled around on his hind legs, still more nuggets were tossed.

Ned shook his head in amusement. "Whaddya say, Nugget? Think you could spin a waltz or two?"

Nugget gave him a disgusted look.

"Come on, then. Let's see what else is going on."

Every corner had a band of one sort or another, with flutes and fiddles, cornets and mandolins, and dozens of street organs vying for attention. And music wasn't the only thing going for entertainment. According to the advertising posters, there was a minstrel show in town, and acrobats. A rodeo was coming, even a show of moving pictures.

As Ned walked farther down the street he heard something he hadn't heard since he'd left home. Could it possibly be a piano? He stopped outside a pair of swinging doors and listened. Sure enough, someone was pounding a tune on a tinny piano. *There is a tavern in the town, in the town ...* Ned hummed along with delight. How they'd managed to haul a piano over the pass was anyone's guess, but judging from the enthusiastic crowd packed inside the saloon, it had been well worth the effort.

He left the piano and strolled over to the Alaska Commercial building, where a large crowd was clustered around the notice board. The board was littered with ads looking for men to cut wood, haul water, dig graves or work in the sawmill or warehouse or brewery. There were plenty of jobs for cooks, too. All you had to know was how to open a can. And there were all sorts of personal messages.

Ned pushed his way to the front and scanned the messages, wondering why his mother hadn't written. She would certainly have received his letter by now. After all, he'd sent it way back in November.

A yellowed sheet of paper, partially hidden by more recent additions, caught his eye. The message was spattered with dried mud, but he could make out *N E R*. Part of Turner? He was reaching out to remove the notice when Nugget gave a low growl. At the same time, Ned felt a strong arm encircling his back.

"How are ya, Buckingham?" Montana's voice boomed in his ear. "Come into town, huh? Fixin' to do a little celebrating? I got just the place, and it looks as though you got the time. Still got that mutt, too, I see. Darn thing never did like me." As he spoke, he was steering Ned away from the notice board and down the crowded street. "How'd ya make out over the winter? You stake a claim and strike it rich?"

"Not yet. I've been working for wages."

Montana snorted. "Some dream, huh? Not quite what you figured. Ah, well. You look pretty good, all things considered. You had enough food 'n' all?"

"I managed," Ned said, then added, "No thanks to you."

"Ahhh ... How about a truce, kid? Let bygones be bygones. Admit it, we helped each other out on that trail. Come on, admit it. Them rapids, the ice jam — I got you through some pretty rough scrapes."

Ned shrugged. "Whatever you say."

By now they'd reached the Blue Spruce Saloon, and Montana was ushering Ned inside. "This is your place?" Ned looked around. Like most of the buildings in Dawson, the fancy wooden exterior was only a front. The inside was nothing more than a tent with a sawdust floor. "It's nice. Now I'd better be going."

"Come on! You must be thirsty after that long walk. Have a drink on the house." He took Ned to a table and sat him down. "Jake!" he called to the barman. "A coupla whiskies over here."

"Not for me," Ned said. "I'll have a ginger ale."

"Ginger ale?" Montana laughed. "Nobody celebrates on ginger ale. Here." He handed Ned a shot glass of whiskey. "Bottom's up, kid. Don't look so worried. One shot ain't gonna kill you." He drained his own glass and ordered another round.

Ned stared at the amber liquid. Why not? He'd turned seventeen in March. He was almost a man, for goodness sake. And he had wages, a man's wages, glittering in his poke. So why not?

"Atta boy!" Montana grinned.

Just then the swinging doors burst open and two bearded prospectors strode in. "Here's who we're waitin' for!" Montana exclaimed. "Buckingham, meet my old friends from Seattle. Freddy the Shirt and Jawbone. They're workin' a claim on Eldorado Creek. This kid here, fellas, he's celebrating months of hard labor. First time in the city for months, ain't that right, Buckingham? Next stop, the dance hall. Good-lookin' kid like you!" Montana slapped Ned on the back and laughed loudly. The others joined in.

Ned laughed self-consciously, hoping his face didn't look as red as it felt. Then he downed his second glass of whiskey and pushed back his chair. "Thanks, Montana, but the bank'll be closed in a few minutes. I've gotta go there, then over to the post office."

Montana and his friends wouldn't hear of it. "You're not walkin' back to the creeks tonight, are ya? Stay and have some fun."

"Gosh, you spent the whole winter working underground, and when you weren't down the hole you were stuck in your cabin talking to that fool dog. Am I right?"

"Stay awhile and see if it don't do you the world of good. There's more folks comin' in, and things'll get pretty lively."

"Well ..." Ned had to admit they were right. He didn't have to hurry back. He could go to the bank tomorrow. Mail the money home, check the post office for letters — all that could be done tomorrow. Before he knew it, he was drinking a third glass of whiskey.

Time ticked away. The smoky room became fuzzy. Faces blurred in and out of focus. Voices swelled in and faded out, rowdy and boisterous, low and despondent. Ned traced them in the air, the sounds rising and falling like waves, slap-slapping against the shore.

Sometime later — a long time later — a roving street band came in with a fiddler, trombonist and drummer. Nugget threw back his head and howled as they started to play.

"That's *Hot Time in the Old Town Tonight!*" Ned leapt to his feet and sang along. When the trombonist finished the piece several bars ahead of the others, Ned applauded vigorously. "Congratulations, Trombone! You won the race!"

It was the last thing he remembered.

. 25 .

How Could This Happen?

Two weeks after Catherine moved in, Sarah's luck took an unexpected turn.

She was in the post office at the time, searching for a letter addressed to a Mr. Campbell. As she was rummaging through the sacks, she was thinking about the block of ice Catherine had ordered, and the glass of wild raspberry cordial that awaited her at the cabin. She was imagining the cold tangy-sweet taste when she came across a letter that made her gasp.

It was the familiar handwriting that first grabbed her attention. Then the name and address — Mrs. Violet Turner, Victoria.

There was no doubt in Sarah's mind. Ned had written the letter.

She waved the stained and crumpled envelope at the mail clerks. "This was mailed out!" she cried. "See, the address is Victoria! What's it doing in the sack coming in?

And look at the postmark. November! It was mailed way back in November!"

"Now, Sarah," the older clerk said. "There's no need to upset yourself."

"But it's addressed to my mother, see? My brother wrote it! Why wasn't it sent? If Mother had got this letter like she was supposed to, she never would've planned to come. And I wouldn't be here, not if she — if, if — Ohh!" She stamped her foot in frustration. "How could this happen?"

The clerks wondered, too. They emptied the sack and discovered dozens of letters, all addressed to places on the Outside. New York, San Francisco, Seattle, Victoria ... All of them postmarked November, 1897.

"Somehow things got muddled," one said. "You want us to mail the letter again?"

"Not till I've read it. I've been waiting for — Ohh! It feels like years." She put the letter in her pocket, quickly sifted through the last mail sack and, after delivering Mr. Campbell's letters, hurried home.

Catherine was hard at work sewing a new shirt for a miner whose own two shirts were ripped and frayed beyond repair. She got up when Sarah entered and immediately went to the ice chest. "You look as though you could use a cold drink," she said. "You're as red as a raspberry."

"It's not the heat, it's — oh, Catherine! You won't believe what's happened. Look at this letter! It does say Mrs. Violet Turner, doesn't it? And Victoria? And here, the return address. The letters are smudged and it's awfully grimy, but you can make out the N — that is an N, isn't it? For Ned. And Grand something. Ohhh! I'm so excited and scared I can hardly think."

Catherine sat her down and handed her a glass of raspberry cordial. "Take your time," she said. "You've been waiting this long, another minute won't hurt. Go on, have something to drink."

"I can't, my stomach's all butterflies. Would you — I'm so nervous. Maybe you should read it? No ... No, it's all right. I can do it."

She took a few deep breaths, then opened the envelope. There were two letters inside, a short one dated November the fifteenth, and a much longer one dated November the twenty-fifth. Sarah began with the latest one.

Grand Forks, November 25, 1897

Dear Mother and Sarah,
I've been thinking long and hard, and it seems to me that every man who got to the Yukon in as good a shape as when he started is a lucky man ...

Sarah stopped and grinned. "Grand Forks! That's not far, is it? And listen, he says he's a lucky man. That's a good sign, isn't it? Let's see what else ...

"Oh no. I've read it wrong. He goes on to say, *but those men that have the luck in the goldfields are few and far between and I cannot count myself among them. If I'd known then what I know now, I never would have undertaken this journey ...*" A worried look scrawled across Sarah's face. "He sounds very depressed."

"Don't worry," Catherine said. "He probably had a few bad experiences, same as the rest of us. But read on. He'll tell you the good news, you'll see. At least now you know where he is."

"You're right." Sarah smiled. "It's just that — I don't know. I'm just so excited!"

There were five pages. Both sides were covered with a cramped version of Ned's handwriting, as if he hadn't wanted to waste a bit of space. He hadn't wanted to spare details, either, no matter how grim or worrisome.

As Sarah read on, her excitement gave way to despair. And by the time she'd finished the letter, she wasn't even sure if Ned had stayed in the Klondike, he sounded that low. He could have left for home the same time she was sailing down the river. Wouldn't *that* take the frosting off the cake.

Well, there was only one thing to do. She had to go to Grand Forks and find this Mr. Thurston Ned mentioned. After that —

No, she wouldn't think that far ahead. She'd take things one step at a time.

. 24 .
A Startling Discovery

July 7, 1898

Once bitten, twice shy. Isn't that what I swore in Skagway? I thought I'd learned my lesson ...

Ned woke with the feeling he'd done something disastrous.

He was lying in a narrow bed, in a grimy hotel room, with no recollection of how he'd gotten there.

His head throbbed. His stomach lurched if he so much as blinked. His mouth and throat felt as if he'd swallowed a bucket of gravel. The only thing close to a comfort was Nugget, who gazed at him with a mournful look.

Ned ventured a groan. "You could tell me a thing or two, couldn't you?" he croaked, then retched with the effort of speaking.

Nugget pulled away the thin blanket and placed a paw over Ned's shirt pocket.

With sudden awareness, Ned bolted to a sitting position. He instantly regretted the move, but neither the hammering in his head nor the churning of his stomach could outweigh the overwhelming feeling of dread. He'd done it again. He'd lost it all. His poke, full of gold, was gone.

"Oh, God!" he cried. "They stole it!" He lurched out of bed, swallowed a half-pitcher of tepid water, then poured the rest over his head. "Montana, the others — I should've known better. I *did* know better. Oh, God, what've I done?"

He'd go straight to the Mounted Police. He'd tell them, he'd tell them about that crook Montana.

He was halfway out the door when he heard a rustling in the back pocket of his trousers. Curious, he reached inside and pulled out some sort of document.

"No ..." he groaned as he started to read. "Oh, no, no!" He rubbed his aching eyes. His head reeled, he had trouble focusing on the words, but one thing was clear. The original names on the paper had been crossed out, and *Ned Turner* written in their place. The paper was signed and stamped by the gold commissioner. It appeared that Ned was the new owner of a claim on the upper Eldorado.

"It's a hoax," he muttered as he stumbled down the stairs. "It can't be real."

A visit to the commissioner's office proved otherwise. It's a legal document, Ned was told. Signed by all parties, including himself.

A smoke-filled memory nudged the back of Ned's mind. A street band. Swaying in time to the music. Standing up and singing ...

He remembered a piece of paper being thrust into

his hand, and someone exclaiming, "The Eldorado! My own claim!" Had that been his voice?

He remembered a bottle of ink and a pen. And trembling fingers ... Had he been able to write? He pointed to the signature. "See that? It's a scrawl! It's not my usual handwriting."

"It's perfectly legal," the commissioner said. "Be proud you were able to sign at all. There's many a stake-holder that marks with an X. Like it or not, you're the owner of a claim. Isn't that what you came here for?"

"But that claim's worthless! I've heard of the upper Eldorado. Frosty Jack and the other old-timers, they all say the timber leans the wrong way. The lay of the land is wrong!"

"Guess that's why the new-timers sold it to you."

"But I wasn't thinking! They took advantage, they did it on purpose!"

The commissioner sighed. "If there was a law against taking advantage or a law against not thinking, three-quarters of this town would be working on the woodpile. There's only one bit of advice I can give you. Either take advantage of someone more gullible than yourself, or get out there and work the claim."

"I'll sell it back," Ned decided as he made his way to the Blue Spruce Saloon. "I'll find those crooks and sell it back."

He didn't get any sympathy from Jake, the barman, nor did he get much information. "They all left when you did," Jake said. "Montana half-carried you outa here. Where you went next ain't no concern of mine. You look a bit peaked, kid. Wanna whiskey?"

Ned clutched his stomach, sick at the thought. He left the Blue Spruce and looked in every saloon along Front Street. When that proved unsuccessful, he started down Second. Then Third. He was looking over the top of the swinging doors at the Red Feather Saloon when he spotted them, all three men, sitting around a gambling table.

"There they are Nugget. This is it." He braced himself against the reek of stale ale, and pushed open the swinging doors. He walked straight to the men, shoved the paper under their noses and said, "I want my gold back."

Jawbone belched noisily. "Deal's a deal, kid. Don't go blamin' us."

"Especially when it was your idea to buy it. You insisted!" Freddy the Shirt maintained. "We tried to talk you out of it, but oh no, you wouldn't take no for an answer. Ain't that right, Montana?"

Montana held out his hands in a what-can-I-do gesture. "'Fraid they're right, kid. You insisted. Emptied your poke right there on the table. Pleaded with them to take it. Heck, you was practically bawling. I come all this way to stake a claim, that's what you said. Freddy the Shirt and Jawbone, they just made your dream come true."

Ned fought to control the rising nausea. He clenched his fists. His eyes hardened.

"You got something else on your mind?" Montana said. "If not, we got a game to play. We'd cut you in, but it don't look like you're much in the running. Unless, of course, you wanna take out a loan?"

"You — !" Ned glared. If only he hadn't been so stupid. Well, now he had to pay the consequences. He straightened his shoulders and thrust out his chin. "All right. If that's the way it is. I better get to work." With as much pride as he could muster, he walked away. But as he opened the swinging doors, something totally unexpected happened.

"STOP!" Montana bellowed. He leapt to his feet, pushed Ned out of the way and stormed into the street. "Cat! Somebody stop that girl! Cat!"

Ned saw a dark-haired girl in a pink calico dress turn and look his way. Her eyes widened with fear as Montana charged toward her.

Ned didn't think twice. Forgetting his throbbing head and queasy stomach, he hurled himself after Montana and knocked him to the ground. Then Nugget bounded in and sank his teeth into Montana's leg.

"Get 'im offa me!" Montana pounded the dog with his fists. "Get 'im offa me!"

"Nugget, that's enough!" Ned cried. "Come on!" He raced up the dusty street and around the corner with the dog fast at his heels. A few steps more and he had to stop, no longer able to ward off the nausea. "Never again," he groaned between spasms. "That's the last time. Ohhh ..."

He leaned against a cabin wall and took a few moments to steady himself. In the distance he could hear Montana shouting over the crowd. "So the leg's bleeding! That's nothin'! Whaddya think I am, some kind of skirt? I'll get that kid! You hear me, Buckingham? I'll have you and that mutt for breakfast! And that girl, too! You hear me, Cat? You're gonna get what's comin'! No use tryin' to hide, I'll find you!"

Montana's supporters cheered him on. From what Ned could make out, two searches were underway. One for Ned and the dog, the other for the girl.

"C'mon, Nugget. We've gotta get away." Ned took a zigzag route up the hillside, along one narrow street and up the next. The farther he was from the center of town, the better. At least until the commotion died down.

He was about to cross another street when a voice behind him called, "Quick, over here!"

Startled, he turned and saw the girl in the calico dress beckoning from a small cabin.

Ned did not hesitate. He ducked under a line of washing, called his dog and slipped inside.

• • •

At first glance, the cabin was not much different than most miners' shacks. It was built of logs and had a sod roof. Inside, there was a sheet-iron cookstove, assorted furnishings and two built-in bunks. A large metal basin and scrub board stood in one corner, and in another corner, a makeshift icebox. Through a narrow doorway, Ned could see a smaller room with a bed and a trunk.

Several unminerly touches set this cabin apart from the ones on the creeks. A hooked rug lay on the rough plank floor. A crocheted tablecloth covered the table. Gingham curtains hung at the two tiny windows. Spare blankets, no longer needed for warmth, had been pinned to the walls, along with pictures of mountain scenes. A china wash basin and pitcher sat on one of the cupboards, while the other was filled with cups and plates.

Someone had gathered a bouquet of wild roses and placed them in a tin can on the table. Ned breathed in the scent and took another look around the cabin. "It's — it's like a home," he stammered. His throat felt tight, his head woozy, and for one dreadful moment he thought he was going to be sick again. "It's — I'm sorry. It's been a long time..."

"Since you've seen a woman's touch?" The girl smiled shyly.

Ned turned away, flustered, wishing he still had a beard to hide his burning cheeks. It wasn't simply "the woman's touch," but the girl herself. Gosh almighty, when was the last time he'd spoken to a girl, let alone a girl as pretty as this one?

"It's not my cabin," she went on, "but you'll be safe here. And thank you. For helping me out."

Ned forced his thoughts back to the matter at hand. "Is he, is Montana — ?" He vaguely remembered a conversation he'd overheard at Lake Bennett. "Is he a relative or something?"

The girl didn't answer, but pulled out a chair and motioned for Ned to sit down. "Would you like something to drink? Some coffee? The weather's a little hot for coffee, but I was heating water to do the laundry. You probably noticed the wash hanging outside. Or I could offer you some cold raspberry cordial. I picked the raspberries myself, mostly off the roof of the cabin."

"Raspberry cordial would be a treat," he said.

The girl poured two glasses, then sat across from him at

the table. "I heard his voice a couple of weeks ago. Montana's voice. When I was working in the dance hall ..." She spoke quietly, with long pauses. "I wasn't sure. I hoped I was imagining things. I kept telling myself, It can't be him, it can't be. When I saw him just now ..."

"Is he, why was he — ?"

"He won me in a poker game. My father had already lost all his money. So he — he put me up instead. Montana won. Said he needed a servant. That was going on two years ago. I was fourteen."

"Your own father?" Ned gasped. "How could he?"

The girl shook her head sadly. "That day, that was the last time I ever saw him. I refused to speak to Montana. It made him crazy."

"Cat. He called you Cat."

"My name's Catherine, but he called me Cat. Partly because I was so quiet. And partly because of the nine lives a cat's supposed to have. Montana did his best to take them away."

There was a long silence. Then Catherine said, "He was coming after me one night, drunk as usual, and furious 'cause the supper wasn't cooked to his liking. And I — I had enough. So I ran away."

She paused for a while, and busied herself rearranging the roses on the table. Then she turned back to Ned. "What about you? How do you know Montana?" A wary look came into her eyes, as if she was suddenly suspicious, and sorry she'd told him so much about herself.

"Don't worry," Ned assured her. "He's not a friend. Not by a long shot." He told her his story, from the moment he met Montana on the steamship to the day they arrived in Dawson. "That's the last I saw of him, until yesterday. But what about you? When you ran away, is that when you came up north?"

"I was in Seattle the day the boat came in with all that gold. But I went south to San Francisco. I was there —"

"Wait," Ned interrupted. "When I was at Lake Bennett with Montana, one of his friends said he saw a girl take the first boat out of Seattle for the Klondike. He must've meant you. That's how Montana knew where you'd gone."

"Montana's friend might've seen me on the wharf that day, but he figured wrong."

"And in San Francisco?"

"I didn't stay there long. I went to Victoria and got a job. But after awhile I got restless. It seemed like everybody was off to the Klondike, so I decided to come, too."

"Victoria?" Ned smiled. "That's where I'm from. And that's why I'm here, a bad case of goldrush fever. For a while I didn't think I'd make it, then just when I got some gold saved up ..." He groaned, and told her about his latest misfortune. "You're looking at one ignorant fool."

"If Montana had a hand in it, you're lucky the gold was all you lost."

"I expect you're right." He fidgeted with the empty cordial glass, wishing he had an excuse to stay longer. "Well ... sounds like things have quieted down out there. I'd better get going. Thanks again, Miss Catherine."

"You're going back to the creeks?"

Ned gave a bitter laugh. "I've gotta go and work my new claim. Say ..." His attention was drawn to a quilt neatly folded on one of the bunks. "That looks like the quilt my mother made for me. She insisted on packing it, kept saying I'd need the warmth. She was right, too. I sure could've used it."

"Did you leave it behind?"

"No, but in Skagway ... this same ignorant fool lost his whole outfit in a poker game. I managed to get it back, but it was missing a few choice items. Like the quilt."

"Take a closer look if you want."

Ned unfolded the quilt, spread it over the bunk and smoothed it with his fingers. "It's exactly the same. No, I'm wrong. Same scraps of material, same colors, but the pieces are laid out differently. Mother told me the name of the pattern, but I don't recall that sort of thing."

"It's called a log cabin," Catherine said. "See the little red square in the center of every block? That represents the chimney or hearth, the center of the home. It's the warmth that holds the family together. And all these other pieces represent the logs, or the home itself."

Ned smiled. "Mother always says, Home is where the heart is."

"Where the *hearth* is. That's what Sarah said when she showed me her quilt."

"What?" Ned suddenly felt as though someone had struck him a blow between the eyes. "What — what did you say?"

"The hearth."

"No, no, I mean the name!" he shouted. "The name!" When he saw that he was frightening her, he lowered his voice and forced himself to speak more calmly. "I'm sorry.

I meant the name of the girl. What did you say it was?"

"Sarah. Sarah Turner. She's from —" A slow under-standing began to show on Catherine's face. "You're from Victoria, aren't you? You said that before, but I didn't make the connection. Oh, heavens, why didn't it sink in? You must be Ned, Sarah's brother! She spoke of nothing else, the whole journey. How desperate she was to find you."

Ned lowered himself on to the bunk, the quilt wrapped in his arms. "It's impossible, she's only twelve. Thirteen now, I suppose, but she couldn't have come — oh, my God." A dreadful thought came to him. Had Mother taken ill, or passed away? Was that why Sarah had come? He swallowed hard. "Is Mother — did my mother — ?"

"No, nothing like that," Catherine assured him.

"But for Sarah to come all this way by herself? Mother wouldn't allow it, for one thing. And Sarah couldn't have made it — she's not that strong."

"Well, she did. She's amazing, your sister. We traveled together, along with the Nickersons, over the Chilkoot Trail. And not a word of complaint from Sarah, not ever. We got here about a month ago. The Nickersons, they're off working a claim, and they left me and Sarah to mind their cabin."

"So where is she now?"

"Oh, Ned. She's gone off to the creeks to look for you."

. 25 .

More Surprises

When Ned asked if Catherine wanted to accompany him to the goldfields, she readily accepted. Not only would she be safe from Montana, she'd also have a chance to visit Mrs. Nickerson. But first she'd see Sarah reunited with her brother.

They left that same afternoon, armed with supplies. Three miles west of Dawson they clambered on to a barge that took them across the Klondike River to the confluence of Bonanza Creek. "It's a lot easier going when it's frozen," Ned said as they started out along the trail. "I can't imagine Sarah traipsing through here. She wasn't by herself, was she?"

"No, she went on horseback with Corporal Murdoch late yesterday afternoon. You must've just missed each other on the trail. She was planning to ask about you in Grand Forks, and find out how to get to your cabin. I expect she's there right now, with a pot of tea on the stove." She laughed. "If there's one thing you don't have to worry about, it's Sarah."

Ned shook his head in amazement. The sister he knew wouldn't have crossed a street in Victoria without weighing the pros and cons. What fool notion had compelled her to go to the Klondike? At thirteen years old, for goodness sake! What was Mother thinking? Didn't she know what Sarah would be facing? Hadn't she read his letter?

When he voiced this out loud, he was shocked by Catherine's answer. "She never got your letter. It somehow got mixed up in the mail system and ended up back in Dawson. Sarah found it by chance, only yesterday. That's how she knew about Thurston's claim, and where you were living. She didn't have a clue before. You could've been dead for all she knew."

And Mother would have feared the same thing. Ned cursed himself for his thoughtlessness. One letter a week, that's what he should have sent. At the very least, one a month. They wouldn't *all* have gone astray.

"Sarah earned quite a bit of gold herself," Catherine went on. "She stood in line for the miners and got their mail. She sold fresh bread on Front Street. And she helped Mrs. Nickerson with the laundry."

"*Sarah?* Mother took in washing after Father died. Sarah never lifted a finger to help." The moment he spoke the words, he realized it wasn't true. Sarah had tried to help, but never to Mother's satisfaction. In the end, Mother had said it was less trouble to do it herself.

"You should have seen how hard she worked," Catherine said. "She was the one who panned the wash water before tossing it out." She laughed at Ned's stupefied expression. "For the gold dust! All those little flakes that get trapped in the pockets and the cuffs. Oh, yes. The gold is wherever you find it. That Sarah, she taught me a few things."

"But to wander around Dawson by herself! Let alone set up a bread stand."

"Ned, did you notice many children in Dawson?"

"Well, no ..."

"There, you see? Neither did the miners. They're lonesome, as well you know. They miss their homes and families. Sarah reminded them of all that. They sort of adopted her, and treated her like one of the family. There's a young singer who affects them the same way. Little Margie Newman. The minute she appears on stage the tears come to their eyes. All those tough, hardened prospectors, they get awful sentimental at times. Sarah doesn't sing, but she's got a smile that breaks their hearts."

How wonderful it will be to see that smile, Ned thought. To think of little Sarah, coming all this way.

"Watch your step!" Catherine exclaimed. She pointed to several high rubber boots sticking out of the mud. "This trail's getting nasty."

Ned grunted in agreement. "Don't know what's worse, picking through the muck when it's frozen or walking through it when it's thawing out. I hope it's not too rough for you."

Catherine tossed her head and scowled. "I appreciate your concern, but I did make it here in one piece!"

"You're right," Ned said. "I'm sorry."

"No, I'm sorry. It's just that — never mind." She hoped he wasn't offended by her outburst. She didn't know how to accept kindness, that was the problem. It was hard enough with the Nickersons and Sarah, but this young fellow ... She'd better concentrate on the trail.

Negotiating the trail needed concentration. The top layer was moss, some two feet thick and soaking wet. In low spots, the water lay in pools across the trail. If they weren't careful, they could sink into mud up to their knees.

They balanced over logs to cross streams and muddy ditches, then climbed up steep hills and along rocky cliffs to avoid the bogs and sump holes. They couldn't avoid the mosquitoes.

When she could stand it no longer, Catherine fished into her bag and brought out the tulle contraption she'd made at Lake Laberge.

Ned laughed when she put it on.

"Laugh now, pay later," she said. "We'll see who ends up with a face still intact."

"That sounds like a wager." Ned reached into his pack, took out a tin can, then dipped in his fingers. Before long he'd smeared a thick black goo all over his face.

Catherine gaped. "What on earth —?"

"A little trick I learned from Frosty Jack. It's a mixture of pitch and lampblack. I could've used grease and soot, but all I've got is bacon grease, and the smell about now wouldn't sit well on my stomach."

"Your sister's going to have a good laugh at the look of you, that's all I can say."

The journey through the goldfields was difficult, but never lonely. They passed numerous bunkhouses and lunch tents, cabins and claims. They made their way around or over the holes and dumps, shining bright with fragments of quartz. They greeted miners working on their sluices. And in every creek, the water was yellow with the dirt from washing the gold.

"Must've been pretty at one time," Ned remarked. "Frosty Jack told me it was all stunted timber, this whole valley, covered with moss and timber. There were lots of birds and butterflies and flowers in the spring, and berries. Moose and caribou, too. Now look at it."

Catherine gazed over the valley. The trees had been cut down. The hills were scarred with long ditches carrying water to the sluice boxes. Piles of dirt and ash and gravel were dumped along the creek beds. The only green left seemed to be the thorny devil's club vine. "It's not a pretty sight," she said. "But nobody came here for the scenery. I guess there's a price to be paid for everything."

• • •

Grand Forks lay at the confluence of Bonanza and Eldorado creeks. Catherine thought it looked shabby with its clapboard storefronts, muddy streets and flimsy boardwalks, but it was unquestionably a thriving town.

It didn't take long to find out about Sarah. They'd no sooner stepped inside the General Store to begin their inquiries when the shopkeeper exclaimed, "Hey, Long Shanks! You just missed your little sister! Came in yesterday with Fred Murdoch, and wouldn't you know it? Frosty Jack and his missus was here at the same time. They took Sarah home with them. Far as I know she spent the night there."

As Ned and Catherine were about to leave, Chilblains

and Skipper walked into the store. "You talkin' about young Sarah?" Chilblains asked. "She's at your place now, Long Shanks. We seen her when we passed by this morning. But you sure that's your sister? Tall and kinda skinny, long brown hair, hazel eyes?"

"Fine-looking girl," Skipper added. "Can't say there's much of a fam'ly resemblance."

"'Specially not with that mug o' yours blacked up with pitch."

Ned laughed and pulled out a handkerchief to wipe his face. "Guess I'll put up with the mosquitoes for a bit."

"Who's this, then?" Chilblains smiled at Catherine and gave Ned a nudge in the ribs. "You get yerself hitched in Dawson? You devil!"

Ned blushed furiously. "She's a friend of Sarah's. Came over the Chilkoot with her and the Nickersons."

"Would that be the Nickersons over on Too Much Gold?" Skipper said. "Met 'em this past week. They're a fine bunch. They come from the same part o' Nova Scotia as me. Next time you see 'em, tell 'em I hope they get lucky. Tell 'em good-bye, too. End of the week, I'm leavin' the Klondike for good. Guess you'll be leavin' too, Long Shanks, you 'n' young Sarah. If you want my advice —"

"Shut yer trap, Skipper," Chilblains laughed. "He don't want advice, he wants to see his sister. Go on, kid, get outa here."

A short time later, Ned's cabin was in sight. A blue plume of smoke rose from the chimney. "Sarah!" Ned cried. "Sarah, are you there? Sarah!"

The cabin door flung open. In no time at all, Sarah

was flying into his outstretched arms. "Oh, Ned, I can't believe it's really you!" She grabbed his hand and pulled him inside. "There's sourdough bread from Mrs. Thurston. And I made a stew with some rabbit Mr. Harris gave me — he's one of the miners I get letters for — and of course there's beans and bacon but you must be sick of that, aren't you? And Catherine! How did you find him? Did he — oh, I'm sorry for rattling on like this but it's just that I'm so, so —" She burst into tears.

Once she'd blown her nose and caught her breath, she said, "You better tell me everything, Ned. Here, Nugget, I know all about you. Come on, there's a good boy." She stroked the dog and listened as Ned and Catherine took turns filling her in on the day's events.

"So, Ned, you've got your very own claim? We'd better get to work!"

"We? You silly goose! You're not planning to work with me. You can't! You're only thirteen!"

"Yes, I'm planning to. And thanks for remembering I'm a year older than I was when you left."

"Sarah, be reasonable."

"Listen here, Ned." Sarah glowered at her brother. "I've hiked over the Chilkoot Pass, I've gone through the rapids, I've been eaten alive by mosquitoes, and I've been more scared than I ever believed possible. I lost the Waverleys in an avalanche and it was a wonder I wasn't buried myself. And — and I was all alone but I made it. And I've written to Mother and told her about your missing letter and where you are and that I'd be helping you out. And don't ever tell me I can't, because I can. You're not —"

Her lower lip began to tremble but she forced back the tears and pressed on. "You're only four years older than me. You're not my father. And you're not my mother. And you could have sent more than one letter!"

Ned held up his hands in a gesture of defeat. "You're right. Let's say we give it some time and see what happens."

• • •

They wasted no time moving Ned's outfit to the upper Eldorado. There they found his new claim, as well as two small cabins built by the previous owners.

Ned told Sarah and Catherine they could have the second cabin, if Catherine wanted to stay. She accepted his offer gratefully. Now that Montana knew she was in the Klondike, he'd never stop looking for her. The farther away she was, the better. In return, she offered to do the cooking and laundry as well as work on Ned's claim.

"You can't!" Ned protested.

"Oh, Ned! There's all sorts of women working on claims. Like Mrs. Nickerson. And Mrs. Thurston, out working on the sluice line. And there's a lady in Grand Forks who staked her own claim, all on her own, and now she's hiring men to help work it."

"All right, you win. But I may not be able to pay you."

"Pay me a percentage."

"I could do that, but a percentage of nothing is still a big zero."

"Have a little faith," Catherine said. "That's what got us here, isn't it? A little faith."

ELDORADO. LOOKING UP FROM NO. 13

. 26 .
Good News

July, 1898

Weather hot and pleasant. Saw a bear and two cubs up on the hill. Frosty Jack brought over some fresh moose meat from his hunting trip. A most welcome treat.

Several days working at the hole. No matter how hard and laborious, it's a fine thing to be working my own claim. Sarah's a trooper and Catherine works as hard as any man ...

When Ned looked over his claim, he saw that the previous owners had managed to dig a fair bit of gravel out of the ground. They'd even washed several loads of it. But they hadn't given the claim much of a chance. "They hardly scratched the surface," Ned remarked. "They didn't even dig to the bedrock." He thought for a moment. "That's what we'll do. We'll dig deeper."

"Don't you want to wash this dump first?" Sarah said. "It seems a shame to be digging underground in the dark, now that there's so much light."

"Nope, I mean to reach the bedrock." Ned was determined. He'd dug out too many rich loads from Frosty Jack's claim not to give his own a chance. "It's just a couple more feet. Catherine, if you can keep the fire going. And Sarah, if you really want to help with the pick ..."

"Sure," she said. "Like Mother always says, Many hands make light work."

In spite of the saying, the work wasn't light. What made it bearable was the hope that their efforts would pay off. And this time the pay would not go to someone else.

One week passed, then two. They were well into the third week when Ned decided to test some of the dirt he'd heaped up. He scooped a load of gravel into his gold pan, poured in the water and began to pan as Frosty Jack had taught him. Tilt the pan, swirl the water, pour off the lighter bits of gravel and sand, and swirl again.

He wasn't hoping for much. Just enough to make it all worthwhile. And wouldn't he love to find a special gold nugget to give to Catherine. One for Sarah and Mother, too, of course. But Catherine! His heart skipped. Who would've thought ...

"Say, kid! How's yer new claim comin' along?"

Ned looked up to see the two former owners approaching, Jawbone and Freddy the Shirt.

"We just come by to see how you was makin' out. Thought you'd've been off to Paris by now."

Ned ignored their jibes. He looked past them down

the trail and wondered if Montana might be following. Nugget must have been thinking the same thing, because he suddenly drew back his lips and growled in a menacing way.

"Shaddup!" Freddy the Shirt shouted. "Gosh sakes, kid, ain't you ever gonna teach this mutt some manners?"

"Nugget, be quiet!" Ned commanded. The dog crouched down but continued to growl.

"Must be a bad smell he picked up," Ned said pointedly. "Something that rubbed off that skunk Montana."

Freddy the Shirt slapped his knee. "If that don't beat all. You hear that, Jawbone? The mutt musta smelt this shirt I'm wearin'. It used to be Montana's, remember? He gave it to me when he took off a few days back."

"He's gone?" Ned asked.

"Got the blue ticket for cheatin' at cards," Jawbone explained. "And a coupla assaults. Yessir, he got shoved on the boat and told to get out of the country and never come back. But don't you worry none, he'll make out all right in Skagway with Soapy and the gang."

"Whaddya talkin' about?" Freddy the Shirt cut in. "Jawbone, you gotta brain like a Swiss cheese. You forget that Soapy got gunned down a few weeks back? Ain't no gang now, unless Montana's fixin' to take Soapy's place. But he don't stand much of a chance, not the way that gang's gettin' rounded up. He's gonna hafta lay low for a spell. Poor ol' Soapy, though. Hey, Jawbone? Shot right on the wharf in Skagway ..."

Ned had stopped listening. Montana was gone! He couldn't wait to tell Catherine. But he had to hear it one more time. "So Montana's left Dawson for good?"

"For good, for ever," Jawbone replied. "Shame, really. He woulda liked to see ya workin' yer new gold mine. Hope the bank'll be big enough. You want some help carryin' it down, all them monumentalish nuggets? We could sell ya a team o' mules if yer stuck!" The men laughed uproariously.

Ned went back to his washing. Let them have their laugh at his expense. He swirled the pan, poured out more gravel, washed in a little more water, swirled — then stopped. "I think I've got some color."

His words provoked a new flood of laughter. "Oh, that's rich!" Freddy the Shirt exclaimed. "You're nothin' but optimicism, kid! Come on, Jawbone. Let's see how the other optimistics are makin' out."

"I do," Ned murmured as the men strutted away. "I do have some color." He swirled, caught another glimpse of color, poured off the gravel, swished the water around — and caught more color, bright gold and gleaming. With trembling hands, he poured off the rest of the water and stared in amazement. Coarse grains of gold glittered in the pan, enough to fill the palm of his hand.

He could scarcely breathe for excitement, but he forced himself to stay calm, at least until Jawbone and Freddy the Shirt were well out of earshot. When their figures were no more than tiny specks way off in the distance, he burst out, "Sarah! Catherine! Come quick! We did it! We did it!"

By the time the girls reached him he was on the ground, waving his legs in the air, all but standing on his head.

"What happened?" Sarah cried. "Are you hurt? Ned, what is it?"

He leapt to his feet, a stupefied expression lighting his face. "Hurt? Did you say hurt?" He jumped in the air like a madman, then grabbed the girls and waltzed them in dizzying circles around the dump. "Strike me, we've done it!" he sang. "Strike me lucky, we've gone and struck gold!"

. 27 .
The Nightmare

Catherine bustled about the small cabin, singing as she packed.

Daisy, Daisy, give me your answer do,
I'm half crazy, all for the love of you ...

She had one more bag to pack. It wasn't proper, staying out on the creek with Ned so close, especially with her feelings taking such a turn. It was new, this giddy, light-headed feeling, and she needed some time and distance to get used to it.

Not that she was going far. With the percentage she'd earned from Ned's claim, she was going to open a dress shop. There were a lot more women in the Klondike now, and they all wanted pretty things, dresses and ribbons and hats and the like. She planned to do some sewing herself, and the rest she would order from Outside. Her very own shop!

And the night before, when Ned had given her the heart-shaped nugget with a promise every bit as precious – Oh, my! She hugged herself with excitement. Truly, Fate had been smiling her way.

The packing done, she decided to make some dumplings for supper, to go with the rabbit stew. She bent down to the flour sack, still singing.

It won't be a stylish marriage,
I can't afford –

Suddenly she stopped. Something was in the doorway, blocking out the sun. She could feel its presence. And without turning around, she knew what it was.

She dropped the cup in the flour and straightened up slowly. The nightmare had found her. And this time, it would not let her go.

"Well, Cat? How many lives now?"

Her heart choked with fear. The same husky voice, roughened by smoke and whiskey. The same menacing tone. *She's worth her weight in gold ...*

The memory dragged her back to a different cabin. One minute she was sitting on a porch eating sun-ripened peaches. The next minute she was kicking, biting and screaming. *No, I won't go! You can't take me away! Papa, make him stop...*

Two minutes, and the Catherine she'd known was gone.

Two years she'd spent, waiting for the nightmare to end. Until that night on the island when he'd struck her with his fist, tearing her skin with his diamond ring. And as he drew back his arm for another blow, she erupted. She reached out to the counter behind her, grappled for a knife, a wooden spoon, anything, and when her hand touched the iron skillet she grabbed it and swung it hard, catching him on the head. He slumped to the floor. She struck him a second time. And he'd lain there, not moving, not breathing ...

"Whatsa matter, cat got your tongue?"

His voice brought her back to the present. "I — I thought —"

He grabbed her and spun her around, forcing her to look into his eyes. "You thought I was dead, didn't you? You thought you killed me. You came pretty close, and we got some score to settle over that."

"I thought — they said you got a blue ticket. You went to Skagway."

"And here I am! Jumped ship, Cat. Hid for a spell. Now I'll head out, but I ain't leavin' the Klondike without you. So whaddya think? You wanna sing about that? Come on!"

"I'm not leaving! Ned —"

"That kid's not gonna help you. He can't even hear you, way off at his sluice line. I hear he got lucky, when was it, a few weeks ago? He ain't no Klondike king, but looks like he's close to a Sir Buckingham after all. Thanks to me. But never mind about that."

"Let me go!" Catherine kicked him hard on the shin.

"Now Cat, you can make it easy or hard, it don't matter to me. One way or another you're comin'."

"I won't go! I won't!" she cried as he pulled her to the door. "You can't —"

"See this?" He stopped, tightened his grip and with his free hand drew a revolver from his coat pocket. "You're gonna come quiet this time." He pointed the gun at her face, then moved it slowly down her cheek, across her shoulder, and pressed it into her back. "Understand?"

She took a sharp intake of breath and nodded.

"Let's go now. Real quiet."

She moved to the door. This wasn't happening. It couldn't be happening. She was leaving the nightmare behind her. She was starting a new life, opening her own shop ...

"Ahh!" A painful twist on her arm forced her back to reality.

"Pay attention, Cat. Just come along nice 'n' slow." He forced her out the door.

She looked past the dumps toward the sluice line. Montana wouldn't go that way and risk being seen. He'd take the long way around, behind the cabin. But then what? "You won't get away with this," she said. "All the miners out here, they know me — you can't get into Dawson without being seen."

"So we wait until dark. It's all been arranged. I got a cabin lined up and my pals are comin' with a wagon —" He stopped abruptly. "Well, well. Ain't this a surprise."

Nugget came bounding around the side of the largest dump. As soon as he caught sight of Montana, he came to a halt and growled, baring his fangs.

Ned and Sarah weren't far behind, and in an instant Ned saw what was happening. "Montana, you scum! Let her go!"

"Try 'n' stop me, kid. Or why doncha sic that mutt on me? Nothin' I'd like better than to finish it off."

"I'll take care of you myself!" Ned stormed forward.

"NO!" Catherine screamed. "He's got a gun!"

Ned was already charging. His fists were clenched, he was ready to fight. He saw a flash of metal, but he didn't stop. He was certain it was a lie, an empty threat, another example of Montana's bullying. The gun wasn't loaded. Couldn't be. And if it was ... too late. He flew in with a punch and hit Montana square on the nose.

Montana hollered with surprise. With the butt of the gun he struck Ned on the side of the head and knocked him to the ground. Then, as Ned was staggering to his feet, he aimed the gun and cocked the trigger. "Don't say I didn't warn you. You wanna call it a draw? Come on, kid. Think of your sister. She is your sister, ain't she? That sweet little thing over there?"

Ned looked over his shoulder. Sarah was only a few yards away, and even though his vision was blurred from the blow, he could see she was badly shaken. Her face was white with shock and her arms were tightly clasped around Nugget. "Sarah," he gasped. "You — Nugget — stay there."

"You see, kid," Montana was saying, "me and Cat, we go back a long ways. She ain't got nothin' to do with you. She's —"

"STOP IT!" Ned summoned all his strength and lunged at the man.

At the same time, Nugget broke free from Sarah's grasp. He tore up the path and with unbridled fury, leapt through the air, straight for Montana's throat.

"No!" Catherine screamed. "Nugget, no!"

The dog slammed into Montana as the gun went off.

. 28 .
A Miracle

August, 1898

All's well that ends well. I've made my decision ...

"It's a miracle no one was killed."

It hadn't taken long for the constable to arrive from Grand Forks. As luck would have it, Frosty Jack had been riding to Ned's with some mail when he heard the gunshot. He quickly assessed the situation, then galloped back to Grand Forks to fetch the Mounted Police.

"Yessir," the constable repeated. "Nothing short of a miracle." He held up the bullet Ned had pried out of the cabin wall. "You take three people and a dog, all close together, and a fourth person a little ways away, and a gun goes off and nobody gets shot? That's a miracle. As for that culprit over there ..." He tossed a scathing look in Montana's direction. "Now we can add illegal possession of a revolver to his substantial list of offenses. He got what's coming. Yessir, he'll be on the steamboat tomorrow, with an armed guard all the way to Seattle."

"Good." Ned looked over at Montana. He was lying in the back of the constable's wagon, firmly tied up and only half-conscious. A cloth was wrapped around his head. "Will he lose his ear?"

"I doubt it," said the constable. "'Course, he's already lost the ear lobe, thanks to that dog of yours. And he'll have one heck of a scar. As for his hearing, from what I can tell that man never listened too good at the best of times."

"Thanks for getting here so quickly," Ned said.

"You got Frosty Jack to thank for that. By the way, congratulations on your claim. Frosty told me all about it, but of course I'd already heard the news. What's your next step? You staying the winter or going Outside?"

Ned paused before answering. It had been a topic of some discussion in the weeks following his strike. He wanted to stay, and it wasn't only because of his claim. As for Sarah, when had she gotten so stubborn? She wanted to stay, too. But they couldn't, not with Mother waiting anxiously at home.

At first he'd planned to sell his claim, go home with the gold, finish his schooling, then go on to university. That's what his father had always wanted.

But he found himself asking, Why? He'd survived that bad spell in the winter. He'd survived the whole winter! That was a miracle in itself. And he liked living in the Klondike. He'd realized that even before he met Catherine.

And she had no desire to leave.

So he'd settled on a compromise. He'd go home for the winter and come back next spring. He smiled. He hadn't even left, and already he was looking forward to coming back.

"That's some smile!" The constable glanced in Catherine's direction, then said to Ned, "I take it you're staying?"

"No," Ned replied. "I'm leaving at the end of August. But as soon as the ice breaks next spring, I'll be back."

. 29 .
Good-bye

"I look different." Sarah turned from side to side, examining herself in the full-length mirror Catherine had set up in her new dress shop. It was the first time in over six months she'd had the opportunity to see her whole self, from head to toe, and she was startled by the change.

She was much taller and more developed, but the changes went deeper than that. Her confidence showed outwardly, in the set of her shoulders and in the way she held her head. It was hard to recognize the timid girl she used to be.

There was something different about her face, too. The mosquito welts had disappeared and the blistering sunburn had healed, but weeks of working under the summer sun, even with a hat, had given her face a rugged glow. Her hands were tanned, and roughened by the hard work and dry air. Mother would have a fit. This wasn't the way a young lady should look. She looked like a prospector! Sarah was secretly pleased.

And her eyes ... The flecks of green looked brighter in contrast with her tanned face, but it was more than the color that struck her. She saw a liveliness that hadn't been there before, a sparkle, an eagerness to embrace whatever happened to come her way. There was knowledge in those eyes. And pride. She had done what thousands of others had done, but what thousands more would never even dream of doing, let alone accomplish. She would have that knowledge, that pride, forever.

Catherine looked up from her sewing just then, and their eyes met in the mirror. "You look different because you *are* different," Catherine said. "Nobody goes through what we went through without changing in one way or another."

Sarah knew the changes weren't only on the outside. Inwardly, she wondered how she could bear going back to school in Victoria, being shut inside a classroom, learning about ancient kings and battles. She'd had her own battles. She'd crossed paths with Klondike kings. Her own brother, while not a king, was at least a duke.

Her heart jumped suddenly. How would Mother react to the new Sarah? And how would Sarah act, once she got back to the comforts of home? She longed to see her mother. But would she lose her sense of independence, her new-found streak of determination?

She had a plan. Only three days ago Ned had received a letter from Mother saying it was a good thing she'd gotten his telegram *this* time — thank goodness Dawson City now had telegraph wires — otherwise, she would have packed her bags and headed to the Klondike herself to find out what was putting her children under such a spell. It couldn't be just the gold.

It's not, Sarah admitted to herself. And when she told her mother about it ... She was certain she could convince her mother to come to Dawson the following spring. She'd *have* to come, if only for Ned and Catherine's wedding. That there was going to be a wedding was perfectly clear in Sarah's mind. You only had to look at the two of them! Her brother wasn't planning to return *just* on account of his gold mine. And it was no accident he was leaving Nugget to keep Catherine company — and to protect her in the unlikely event Montana showed up again.

Of course, Ned didn't know that Sarah was determined to return. And if Mother agreed to come ...

They'd come back in style, that was certain. A railroad was being built over the White Pass. They could take the train all the way to Lake Bennett, then go by steamboat.

As for Dawson itself, Sarah would tell her mother about the school that was opening, and how she wouldn't get left behind in her studies if they decided to stay. And she'd tell her about the church that was going to be built, and the socials. Mother would love it.

"What are you grinning about, Sarah?" Ned appeared in the doorway just then, and set down two heavy suitcases. "You look like the cat that swallowed the canary."

Sarah caught the look that passed between her brother and Catherine, and laughed. "You should talk."

Ned blushed and bent down to adjust the strap on one of the suitcases. When he straightened up he said,

"Well ... are you ready, Sarah? The steamboat's waiting. The Nickersons and Thomas and your miner friends — there's a whole bunch of folks at the wharf, all wanting to say good-bye." He added pointedly, "To you."

Sarah understood. She left Ned and Catherine to say their own good-byes, and hurried down to the river. The sun was shining, the air was warm, the sky was as blue as a chip of new paint. It was still summer. But on the far hillside, the leaves of the birch and aspen had already turned to gold.

photo: John Richthammer

Julie Lawson was born and raised in Victoria, BC. A former elementary schoolteacher, she has written twenty books for young people. Her ideas come from memory and experience, found objects, historical events, a love of language and a potent imagination.

Since childhood Julie has loved writing stories. But she didn't begin writing seriously until 1990. Her first picturebooks included *A Morning to Polish and Keep*, *Kate's Castle* and the award-winning *The Dragon's Pearl*. Julie's first novel, *White Jade Tiger*, won the prestigious Sheila Egoff Award in 1994, and over the past ten years she has garnered many awards and much recognition.

Julie now divides her time between writing at home and visiting schools and libraries. Her travels have taken her as far north as Inuvik, as far south as Perth, Australia, and as far east as St. John's, Newfoundland. She has spoken to round-table groups, toured for Canadian Children's Book Week, conducted writing workshops, taught university courses on writing children's literature and been a presenter at conferences for adults and children across North America.

Julie's life as an author has opened the door to many exciting opportunities, the most recent being writer-in-residence in Dawson City, Yukon. She lived in Pierre Berton's childhood home, now known as the Berton House Writer's Retreat. While enjoying her northern experience, Julie worked on several writing projects, including *Destination Gold*!

Julie enjoys hiking, birding, eating pizza and reading. Her favorite pastime is panning for gold nuggets — in the form of ideas that will one day turn into stories.

The following photographs were provided by the Special Collections Division, University of Washington Libraries:

photographs by Hegg: pg 4 (neg. no. 1391); pg 31 (neg. no. 181); pg 50 (neg. no. 229); pg 84 (neg. no. 777); pg 146 (neg. no. 2267); pg 193 (neg. no. 13B).

photograph by Cantwell: pg 114 (neg. no. 46).

photograph by Child: pg 129 (neg. no. 6).

The photograph on page 160 was supplied by the Vancouver Public Library, Special Collections (VPL 32866).